SECRET AGENT

JASON MASON

AND THE

DASTARDLY

MASTER OF

DISGUISE

SECRET AGENT

JASON MASON

AND THE

DASTARDLY

MASTER OF

DISGUISE

JASON GUNN AND
ANDREW GUNN

BATEMAN
BOOKS

To our beautiful families:
Kathryn, Julia and Emily.
Janine, Eve, Grace, Faith and Louis.
Thank you for always being there for us —
our best stories are all about you.

Text © Jason Gunn and Andrew Gunn, 2024

The moral rights of the authors have been asserted.

Typographical design © David Bateman Ltd, 2024

Published in 2024 by David Bateman Ltd,
Unit 2/5 Workspace Drive, Hobsonville,
Auckland 0618, New Zealand
www.batemanbooks.co.nz

ISBN: 978-1-77689-112-2

A catalogue record for this book is available from the National Library of New Zealand.

Book illustrations and design: Cheryl Smith
Printed in China through Asia Pacific Offset Ltd

MIX
Paper | Supporting
responsible forestry
FSC® C012521
FSC
www.fsc.org

'Remember **Jason**,' said *Colonel Croûton*, 'if you fall from here, there will be no safety rope. There will be no bungee cord. There will only be the small **EMERGENCY** parachute in your backpack.'

'Do the small **EMERGENCY** parachutes always work?' I asked *Colonel Croûton*. She smiled and said, 'No one has ever **complained**.'

We were standing in a very small room with no windows but lots of wires and cables and pipes. *Colonel Croûton* was wearing the uniform of the **Gendarmerie** nationale, which is *French* for 'the police'. I was wearing shorts and a T-shirt that my mum had bought me at Farmers. But that wasn't important because I was about to be invisible.

Colonel Croûton's two-way radio crackled. She talked into it, saying something in French, then 'Jason Mason' and then something else in French.

I wished I understood French. The only French words I was sure of were 'merci' (which means 'thank you') and 'CROISSANT' (which means 'CROISSANT').

'Stand by, Jason, I am opening the access,' said Colonel Croûton. She pulled a lever and right above me a hatch slid open with a CLUNK. I could see blue sky through the hole.

There was a ladder between us. *Colonel Croûton* nodded at me, and I started to climb. When I reached the hole, I **peeped** out and looked around.

Stretched out way below me in every direction was the city of *Paris*. Yes — *Paris*, the capital of France! And everywhere I looked there were old buildings. Some of them I recognised because I'd seen them on TV. But there was one I couldn't see at all: the most **famous** landmark in all of France — the Eiffel Tower.

But don't worry. The Eiffel Tower had not been **STOLEN** by an **EVIL** supervillain. It hadn't moved at all. It was right beneath me. Because at that moment *Colonel Croûton* and I were at the almost-very-top of the Eiffel

Tower. Above where the elevators go. Above where the tourists stand and point. And we weren't there for the view.

'Good luck, **Secret agent Jason Mason**,' said *Colonel Croûton.* 'And remember, the future of a million *French* toilet bowls and all the people sitting on them depends on you.'

I nodded. It was time to start climbing.

I know what you're thinking. Well, actually, I don't know for sure what you're thinking.

You might be thinking, 'I have just found out that Australia is **wider** than the Moon and I have to tell someone, because that is **huge**.'

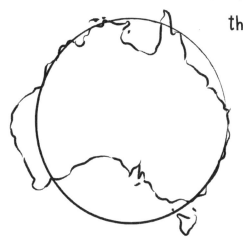

Or you might be thinking, 'How did that much **earwax**

fit inside my ear, and what am I supposed to do with it now?' (These are the sort of things that I often end up thinking.)

I'm thinking, though, that you just might be thinking, 'Wait! **Jason Mason**? Is this the **Jason Mason** from Beardsmore Normal School, who is also secretly a **secret agent** for the New Zealand government? Is he really going to climb to the very top of the Eiffel Tower while invisible? Shouldn't he be in class? What was that about one million *French* toilet bowls?' And also, 'I bet it's cold and *windy* up there — does he have a jacket?'

To be fair, that last question is the sort of thing that only my nana asks. But the answers are:

1. Yes, he is.

2. Yes, he is.

3. No, because it's the school holidays.

4. It's a long story.

5. No, he doesn't have a jacket because it would get in the way of his emergency parachute. But don't worry, Nana, it's a warm sunny day in *Paris*, so even if Jason falls off the top of the Eiffel Tower he won't catch a chill.

Now, if it seems perfectly normal to you that this should all be happening to an eleven-year-old boy from Beardsmore Normal School in Wellington, New Zealand, then you've probably read the first book about my adventures, called **Jason Mason** and the World's Most Powerful ITCHING Powder, or maybe the second book about my adventures, called **Jason Mason** and the Flightless Bird Fiasco. Or maybe both.

If you haven't read them, I **STRONGLY** suggest you go and do that right now. I'll wait here.

Finished?

Just kidding. You don't need to read those books before this one.

I'll tell you **everything** you need to know. That way, as my best friend Kyle says when he takes their family **poodle** Francine and a plastic bag out for a walk, you can just pick it up as you go along.

So, let's go back to the beginning of this story, because it doesn't really start with me being **worried** about falling off the Eiffel Tower. It starts back when my biggest **problem** was having a **secret** that I couldn't tell my best friend. And if you don't know what that **secret** is, you're about to find out.

By the way, Australia really is **wider** than the Moon. I told you it was **huge!**

There are some things it is difficult to tell your friends. Even so, often the best time to tell them is as soon as you can. If your friend has a **BOGEY STICKING OUT** their left nostril, telling them about it could be a problem. But if you wait, it just gets harder — the problem, I mean, not the **BOGEY** — because then your friend will want to know why you didn't tell them earlier.

The **GOOD NEWS** was that my best friend Kyle wasn't going to say,

'Why didn't you tell me that I had a **BOGEY** sticking out my left nostril?'

The bad news was that Kyle might say, 'Why didn't you tell me that, before he died, your great uncle Bill invented a ring that turned you invisible for fifty-eight seconds and that the Prime Minister of New Zealand made you a **secret agent** and sent you on secret missions to stop the **EVIL** villain **Hugh Jarse** exploding a can of the world's most powerful **ITCHING** powder and stealing the plans for the Kiwi 1 space rocket? Also, is his name really **Hugh Jarse?**'

WORLD'S MOST **POWERFUL** ITCHING POWDER

By the way, if you haven't read **Jason Mason** and the World's Most Powerful **ITCHING** Powder or **Jason Mason** and the Flightless Bird Fiasco, you might want to take a look at that last paragraph again. It sums up most of what has happened in my life over the past few weeks. Obviously, it leaves out a lot of details about all the thrills, spills, **hijinks**, laughs and capers, but if you want to learn to about those then you know where to find them.

(**Note:** when I say 'capers' I mean 'unusual or entertaining **escapades**'. A 'caper' is also a very small, **pickled** vegetable used to flavour pasta dishes, but my life over the past week few weeks has not included any of those type of capers.)

Anyway, I have still not told Kyle about my

secret agent life. I was going to tell him at the end of my last book but (as you might remember if you have read it) I was **suddenly** called away on another *URGENT* secret mission. If you're wondering why I haven't written another book all about that urgent secret mission, well, it was a **FALSE ALARM** — and a book called *Secret agent Jason Mason and The Invasion of Alien UFOs That Turned Out To Be Just Some Weird-Shaped Clouds* that was only two pages long would not be much **fun**.

But now I was going to tell Kyle. Even though I had promised not to tell anyone about my **secret** double life, I owed Kyle big time. He had agreed to pretend to be me when I was told to guard Pixie, the pet dog of astronaut Burke Steel, so I could chase down the **EVIL** villain **Hugh Jarse**. He had done it without me explaining to him what was really going on. He trusted me because we were *best friends*, and now I was going to have to trust him back.

The only problem is that when you tell a person a big **secret**, even though they have promised to keep it a **secret**, it might be so big that they blurt it out anyway.

I had a solution to that problem. I would tell Kyle in a place where no one else could hear his reaction.

I would tell him at the top of the **TOWER OF TREMBLES**.

Sometimes a carnival comes to Wellington, where I live. This carnival has two of my favourite things: hot dogs on sticks with tomato sauce and a ride called the **TOWER OF TREMBLES**.
The **TOWER OF TREMBLES** is fifteen storeys high, or about as high as an Olympic-sized swimming pool would be if you **TIPPED** it up on its end (which would be silly because all the water would fall out). There are seats at the

bottom of the **TOWER OF TREMBLES**, which are pulled slowly up to the top. Then the seats are let go and they fall fast back to the ground, slowing down just before they hit it.

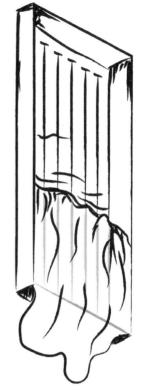

Now, I've fallen further than the length of a tipped-up Olympic-sized swimming pool before. I have skydived out the back of a Royal New Zealand Air Force transport plane, and I have re-entered Earth's atmosphere in a space capsule. But I still think that the **TOWER OF TREMBLES** is a cool ride, and Kyle and I didn't mind waiting twenty minutes in the queue to have a go on it. And, most importantly, when I told him my secret way up at the top, no one would be able to hear us.

As we waited, the seats of the **TOWER OF TREMBLES** dropped with a WHOOSH, and we could hear all the people on board screaming.

'Cool,' said Kyle.

We finally made it to the gate at the front of the queue. There were just two seats on the **TOWER OF TREMBLES**, so it was our turn next. I looked way up to the top and—

'Hey, what's going on?' said Kyle. 'Who's that **clown**?'

As the last two riders had got off their seats, someone else had got on! A **clown**! An actual **clown** from the carnival, with a big red nose, white face, big orange hair, a yellow top and purple-and-white striped pants. And **big** red shoes.

'Where did they come from?' I said.

'I don't know,' said Kyle, 'but they jumped the queue!'

'**Hey** — they jumped the queue!' I said to the ride attendant.

She **shrugged**, opened the gate then said, 'There's one more seat . . .' She pointed at me, and added, '**for you.**'

'I'm not getting on without him!' I said.

'He's not getting on without me!' said Kyle.

But the attendant said, 'Kid, you need to get on,' then (when Kyle wasn't looking) she **raised** one eyebrow in a way that suggested Something Serious Was Going On.

'They're waiting for you,' the attendant added, and pointed to the bottom of the **TOWER OF TREMBLES**. There was another attendant standing there in a colourful carnival attendant uniform. She had her hands on her hips in a way that said **Hurry Up, I Haven't Got All Day.**

It was Agent Rātana.

Agent Rātana, who had taught me everything I knew about being a **secret agent**.

And who I had worked with to defeat **Hugh Jarse**, not once but **TWICE**. And who now appeared to have a part-time job as a carnival ride attendant.

I jogged over to Agent Rātana. From behind me, I heard Kyle say, **'I can't believe this!'**

'Agent Mason,' Agent Rātana said, nodding at me as I climbed into the empty seat on the **TOWER OF TREMBLES**.

'What's going on?' I mumbled as she pulled the safety arms over me.

'Just listen **carefully**,' she said then stepped away.

'What does that even mean?' I said.

I listened, but all I could hear was Kyle shouting 'Unfair!' and 'Boo!'

There was a **CLANK** and **WHIRR** and the **TOWER OF TREMBLES** seats slowly started moving, heading straight up.

I look at the clown beside me, who should have been Kyle. Behind the **big** red nose and under the big orange hair there was something familiar.

'**Jason Mason**, what an unexpected surprise. Well, for you anyway . . .'

It was the Prime Minister.

5

'Isn't this a **brilliant** *disguise?*' said the Prime Minister. 'It means I can get out among the ordinary people and hear what they really think, and nobody notices me.'

I was thinking that ordinary people might actually notice a **clown** quite a lot at anything other than a carnival, but the Prime Minister was talking again.

'Now, I have something **top secret** to tell you.'

'Really? Here?' I said.

'Wouldn't you agree that if you had something top secret to tell someone there would be no better place than the **TOWER OF TREMBLES**?' said the Prime Minister.

For a second, I wondered if the Prime Minister had somehow discovered my plan to tell Kyle. Maybe I had been *sleep-walking* and sleep-talking and had fallen on my phone and accidentally **butt-dialled** the Prime Minister. Or maybe I was over-thinking it.

'Wouldn't your office be a better place?' I asked.

'My office is being debugged,' said the Prime Minister.

'Wow!' I said. 'You mean **FOREIGN SPIES** have planted tiny recording devices?'

'No,' said the Prime Minister, 'I mean it's full of

creepy-crawly bugs. One of them creepy-crawled right up Major Flatly's **trouser leg**.'

'Eeww! That wouldn't have been enjoyable,' I said.

'No,' said the Prime Minister. 'That poor **bug**. And Major Flatly didn't like it either.'

We were now halfway up the **TOWER OF TREMBLES**. Down below on the ground, left behind, I could see Kyle looking up at me with a sad expression, like he had accidentally let go of a **helium balloon**.

'Anyway,' said the Prime Minister, 'I need you to go to Paris.'

'Paris, France?' I gasped.

'Of course Paris, France,' said the Prime Minister. 'What other Paris is there?'

I wanted to say that there was a Paris in Panama and a Paris in Denmark and a Paris in Texas, and also a mountain called Paris Peak in Antarctica, but

I sensed that the Prime Minister may not need this information immediately.

'There is a **MAJOR** security emergency unfolding in Western Europe, and your particular set of *skills* are needed. Agent Rātana and you will travel to *Paris* via London—'

'London, England?'

'Yes, London, England!'

I decided not to explain that there were twenty-nine Londons in the world.

The Prime Minister continued: 'And from there you will report to **BURP**. Agent Rātana will give you further details. That is all.'

We had reached the top of the **TOWER OF TREMBLES**. With my legs dangling in mid-air, I could see lots of Wellington which was fairly amazing. And I was going to *Paris*, France, which was really **AMAZING**. But the one thing I couldn't stop thinking was, 'Did the Prime Minister just tell me to report to **BURP**?'

If you're thinking, 'Yes, I wondered that myself when I read that just now,' then keep reading, and I promise your **BURPY** questions will be answered.

'Well, that is quite the view,' said the Prime Minister, 'but it's time to go down.'

I **braced** myself for the sudden feeling of air **RUSHING** past my ears and my stomach in my mouth. Instead, our seats started moving slowly back towards the ground . . . really slowly. So slowly it was like it wasn't the **TOWER OF TREMBLES** but the Tower of Turtles.

'I don't like sudden drops,' said the Prime Minister, 'so we're going to do this my way.'

Oh great. I hadn't got to tell Kyle. And now I had to make small talk with the Prime Minister all the way down to the ground.

At that moment, I looked down and saw Kyle looking up and looking **puzzled**. That was when I realised I might be able to solve both of these problems at once.

By the way, there is a famous saying about *solving* two problems at once. It is 'to kill two birds with one stone'. But what kind of person throws stones at birds then makes up a saying about it? Well, after checking with **thesaurus.com**, I can tell you it would be a 'REVOLTING', 'BEASTLY' and 'OBNOXIOUS' person, so I will stick to saying that I was about to solve two problems at once.

That was because I had realised that the 'attendant' who had let me through the gate wasn't really a carnival attendant at all. First, she had known what was going on with the Prime Minister. Second — unlike a real carnival attendant — she hadn't told me to leave my phone behind before I went on the **TOWER OF TREMBLES** ride, so I hadn't. It was still in my pocket.

We were descending very slowly. There was plenty of time for me to do this.

'Look, there's the *Beehive*,' I said as I pointed towards a building in the distance. 'Is that your office?'

The Prime Minister looked towards the *Beehive* and started saying something about how if I worked hard, I could have an office like that one day.

Meanwhile, I **wiggled** my phone out of my pocket,

muted it, hit Kyle's name, then slid it back into my pocket.

As the Prime Minister turned back to face me, I looked down and saw Kyle look at his ringing phone.

'So, Prime Minister,' I said, 'you know how I promised to keep everything **s e c r e t**?'

'That's where the '**s e c r e t**' in '**S e c r e t   a g e n t**' comes from,' said the Prime Minister.

I looked down and saw Kyle **frowning** as he listened to our conversation on his phone.

I kept going. 'Yes, well, about that. I have this best friend called Kyle.'

'Would that be Kyle, who phoned you in my office on the day we first met? The Kyle who told you that his pet **poodle** Francine, who had been **CONSTIPATED**, was constipated no longer? That Kyle?' asked the Prime Minister.

Wow! The Prime Minister had a good memory. Although I suppose when you are the Prime Minister there aren't many times when a schoolboy in your office talks about his friend's **poodle's** POOP problems.

I looked down. Kyle was staring up at us with the phone held **TIGHT** to his ear.

'Yes, that Kyle,' I said. 'I was just thinking, it'd be so good to tell Kyle about how you're such a great leader.'

'Well, I am a **GREAT LEADER**, and more people should know that. But I'm afraid you can't tell Kyle that. You **CAN'T** tell him anything about how you know me.'

'Not even—'

'**NOPE. NOTHING**,' said the Prime Minister. 'You can't tell Kyle (one) that your great uncle Bill was a **secret agent** or (two) that he invented a ring that makes you invisible. You can't tell him (three) that you're now a **secret agent** or (four) that you're using your powers of invisibility to defeat EVIL bad-doers. And while I think about it, you can't tell him (five) about the EVIL villain Hugh Jarse. No one needs to know anything more about the Hugh Jarses of this world.'

Job done.

I glanced down at Kyle. His eyes were so wide they were just about **popping** out of his head.

'I understand, Prime Minister,' I said, 'and I promise that Kyle will not find out about this from me.'

'You make sure of that,' said the Prime Minister. 'Anyone who let that sort of information slip out would be in very **serious trouble** indeed. Well, here's my ride. Goodbye, Agent Mason.'

The seats **shuddered** to a standstill when we reached the ground and Agent Rātana appeared beside us. She pulled the safety arms up off us as a brightly-coloured **clown** car pulled up, driven by another brightly-coloured clown, who was hunched over the steering wheel. Even though this **clown** had a **huge** grin painted on its face, it did not seem to be very happy.

The Prime Minister jumped off the **TOWER OF TREMBLES** and into the clown car, then said to the driver, 'Thank you, Major Flatly. To the *Beehive!*'

Yes, the driver was Major Flatly (who I used to call **Major StinkyBreath**), the Prime Minister's head of security and (today only) a **clown** driving a **clown** car.

The clown car puttered away with a **'toot-toot!'** sound like a *squeezy* rubber horn makes.

As we watched it go, Agent Rātana said 'Well, I've always wanted to see *Paris*.'

There was a lot happening — but at least now Kyle knew my big **secret**.

6

'That's the biggest pile of **bullpucky** I've ever heard!' said Kyle.

This was not going as well as I had expected.

We were standing by the sideshows in front of a row of those plastic **clowns** with the open mouths that you stick **ping-pong** balls in. I had expected Kyle to be all

'Wow!' and 'A **secret agent**!' and 'This explains all the weird stuff that's been going on.' And maybe also, 'What's it like being invisible?' But he was not like that at all.

'Look,' I said, 'I know that didn't look like the Prime Minister on the **TOWER OF TREMBLES**.'

'No, no, no,' said Kyle. 'That bit is also a pile of bullpucky. But it's not the biggest pile of **bullpucky**. The biggest pile of bullpucky is the "your powers of invisiblity" bit. Why would anyone say that?'

'Because it's true!' I said.

The row of plastic **clowns** slowly turned their heads back and forth like they were saying, '**Jason, Jason, Jason**, you really didn't think this through, did you?'

'If it's true then prove it,' said Kyle. 'Go invisible right now.'

'Why can't you just believe me?' I said.

'Why can't you just believe I've got **Dumbo** the Flying Elephant hidden down the back of my pants?' said Kyle.

'That would be *RIDICULOUS*,' I said.

'Exactly,' said Kyle. 'Exactly. Wait, wait . . . is someone videoing this? Am I being **pranked?** Is that what this is? That's it. I'm going!'

He turned and walked away.

Just for the record, it was obvious he did not have **Dumbo** the Flying Elephant hidden down the back of his pants.

The row of **clowns** kept slowly shaking their heads. **Jason, Jason, Jason** . . .

Just then I remembered someone Great Uncle Bill had told me about — a man called Carl Sagan. He had been a famous **ASTRONOMER**. He once said that there were more stars in the universe than all the grains of sand on all the beaches on Earth. That is an **AMAZING** fact, but it was not the reason I remembered Carl Sagan right then. It was because he said something else famous. He said: 'Extraordinary claims require extraordinary evidence.'

Here is an example: if I told you that my dad's old-style Volkswagen **Beetle** car had the engine in the back instead of the front, you might say 'Okay **Jason**, that sounds a bit unusual but I believe you and you don't have to show me.'

But if I told you that my dad's old-style Volkswagen **Beetle** car was also a submarine and could travel underwater at **speeds** of eighty-eight kilometres an hour with the windows up, you would probably say, 'Sure, Jason, I'll believe that — when I see it happen,' because that would be an **Extraordinary** Claim.

It made sense that Kyle would ask me to prove that I could become invisible. I would have to show him. He would only believe it when he saw it — or didn't see it. Oh, you know what I mean.

Meanwhile, I still had to figure out how I was going to go all the way to Paris without my parents, and without my parents even knowing.

'We've **won** a family trip to *Paris*! We're leaving tomorrow!' said my mum.

I had just biked home from the carnival and she had a GIANT suitcase open on the dining table and was folding clothes into it.

'We what?!' I said.

'You entered that competition on *Cruisy FM* — with the Breakfast Zoo Morning Team.'

I'm sure you won't be surprised when I tell you I hadn't entered that competition on *Cruisy FM* with the Breakfast Zoo Morning Team at all.

'Don't tell me you've forgotten, you lovely, *thoughtful* boy,' said my mum, and I could honestly tell her that I hadn't forgotten (because you can't forget doing something that you haven't done).

It turns out that to win the competition you had to message **Cruisy FM** and tell them why you wanted your family to go to *Paris*. Someone called **'Jason Mason'** had messaged saying he wanted his family to go to *Paris* because his mum and dad had saved up to go there after they got married — but they never did because his dad was bitten by a *meerkat*.

The Breakfast Zoo Morning Team had rung up my mum to ask if that was really true, and she said it was. The Breakfast Zoo Morning Team wanted to know if it had happened at the place my mum and dad had had their wedding, so they asked my mum where my dad had been bitten.

My mum misunderstood the question and said, 'On the **bum**,' which was also true.

In fact it was all true, apart from me messaging *Cruisy FM*. I had nothing to do with it, but I suspected that the Prime Minister did. And now we were all going to *Paris*.

'*Bonjour*, mon merveilleux fromage!' said my dad, as he walked in holding his phone in front of him.

He explained that he had just downloaded a learning-French app. I later found out that he had just said, 'Hello, my wonderful CHEESE!' to me. He had a lot of learning *French* to do before we left.

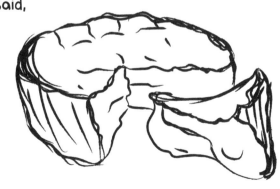

'I knew that getting bitten on the **bum** by a *meerkat* would pay off one day,' my dad continued. 'As the *French* say, chaque nuage a une taie d'oreiller argentée.'* [* translation: 'Every cloud has a silver pillowcase.']

He went on to explain that check-in would be at 7pm tomorrow, but he wanted to be at the airport by 4.30pm just to be on the safe side. When it came to travel, my dad was very organised.

I was still getting my head around going to actual *Paris*, France, when my dad said one more thing.

'One more thing. I've been doing some research into France, and there was something **strange** in the news, in Burgundy.'

Burgundy is a place in France. It is also the name of a famous *French* drink, which I thought was **strange** enough.

It would be like having a place in New Zealand called Coke Zero Sugar.

Anyway, my dad was now talking about a toilet bowl in the middle of a field in Burgundy.

'And it just **disintegrated**,' he said.

'What do you mean, **disintegrated**?' I asked.

'It turned to dust, leaving nothing but a hole in the ground.'

'That is **strange**,' I said. 'Does anyone know what happened?'

My dad shook his head. 'The *French* police are looking into it. But they haven't got to the bottom of it.'

I checked my dad's face to see if this was one of his notorious **dad jokes**. He was completely serious.

A **disintegrated** toilet bowl. In France. Did this have anything to do with my new mission?

I think we both know the answer to that question.

8

The next morning, I was supposed to be packing a bag to go on a **top-secret** mission (and family holiday) to *Paris*, France that very afternoon. Instead, I was sitting on a park bench holding two orange chocolate-chip **ice-creams**, and one of them was beginning to drip.

This was the second thing I had to do today (apart from packing). The first thing was to visit my nana, who is my mum's mum, who had just moved here from the *Shady Acres Rest Home and Villas* in Dunedin.

My nana was now living in the Twilight Views Rest Home and Villas, just around the corner from our house. I took her a packet of Cameo Crèmes, which were her favourite biscuits.

She has a nice room with its own bathroom and a sliding door out to a garden, and a TV with Sky Sports. 'It's like a PRISON,' she said.

I had not seen inside a prison, well not yet **(SPOILER ALERT!)**, but I was fairly sure this was not what one looked like.

'It's not a very good PRISON, Nana,' I said. 'Look, you could get out that door and over the fence before they let the guard dogs loose.'

My nana chuckled and said, 'Not with my dicky knee.'

I told her I would send her some photos of Paris.

'Yes, *Paris*!' she said. 'Your mum and dad were going to go to *Paris* after their wedding, but your dad got bitten on the **bum** by a hippopotamus.'

It was a *meerkat*, as you know, but I just nodded.

'Your great uncle Bill loved *Paris*,' my nana said. 'He went there once. Something to do with the Ministry of Government Departments.'

Great Uncle Bill was my nana's brother. I bet she missed him, too. I wondered what it must have been like to have a brother you never knew was a top-secret agent.

'**Wow!**' I said.

My nana gave me a big wink and said, 'Whiffy cheese!'

I had no idea what that meant, but that was my nana. I gave her a **kiss** on the cheek and said, 'See you when I get back from France.'

She said, 'Buon viaggio!', which I later

discovered means 'Have a good trip!' in Italian.

And now I was doing the second thing I had to do that morning — sitting on a park bench holding two orange chocolate-chip **ice creams**.

Just as I was beginning to think that this was a bad idea, I saw Kyle. He had Francine the **poodle** on a leash. I knew he walked her in the park every day. Good old reliable Kyle.

'Hey, Kyle!' I said. '**Ice cream**?'

He looked at me and I could tell his brain was working out what to do. On the one hand, he was probably still mad at me, but on the other hand: orange chocolate-chip **ice cream**.

He sat down on the other end of the bench and took the cone that wasn't *dripping*.

'Thanks,' he said.

There were a few seconds of silence while I tried to lick all the drips off my ice cream, but I still managed to blob bits of it on my T-shirt, then Kyle said, 'I still don't believe you about all that invisibility bullpucky.'

I decided that all the other stuff apart from the invisiblilty **bullpucky** — like the fact that Kyle's hero Captain Burke Steel had sat on this

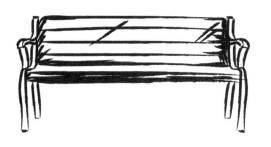

exact park bench after I had landed right beside it in the **KIWI 1** space capsule after orbiting the Earth (see my second book) could wait until later.

'Sure,' I said, 'and you're right. I need to prove it to you. **Extraordinary** claims require extraordinary evidence.'

Kyle nodded thoughtfully. 'Kyle Sagan,' he said.

I decided not to tell him it was actually Carl Sagan and held up my free hand, the one with Great Uncle Bill's ring on it.

'The invisiblilty comes 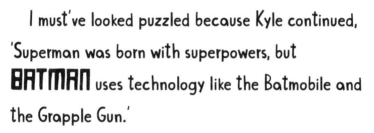 from this ring,' I said. 'Great Uncle Bill gave it to me.'

'So you're more like Batman than **SUPERMAN**,' said Kyle.

I must've looked puzzled because Kyle continued, 'Superman was born with superpowers, but **BATMAN** uses technology like the Batmobile and the Grapple Gun.'

He was right. 'Yes! I'm like Batman . . . or **IRONMAN**.'

Kyle took another bite of his **ice cream** and didn't reply.

It occurred to me that comparing myself to Batman and Ironman out loud didn't sound very cool.

Kyle looked across at my hand. 'It doesn't look like

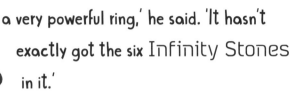

a very powerful ring,' he said. 'It hasn't exactly got the six Infinity Stones in it.'

Kyle was talking about Thanos's Infinity Gauntlet, which was not a ring at all, but I think he knew that.

'I'll show you,' I said, and went to take the ring off using my other hand — the hand holding the melty orange chocolate-chip **ice cream** cone. Which I dropped, of course, and then I dropped the ring, which landed in the melty **ice cream** on the ground.

Then Francine the **poodle** raced in and gobbled it all up . . . including the ring.

'Whoa! No!' I shouted.

'Francine! No!' snapped Kyle.

But Francine just sat there with a **goofy** expression her face.

'My ring!' I said.

'My dog!' said Kyle. 'Why did you give it to her?'

'I didn't give it to her!' I said. 'It just landed on top of the **ice cream**.'

'Oh, yeah?' said Kyle. 'Try telling that to a dog — the thing on top of the **ice cream** is not for eating.'

'I need my ring — for my next **MISSION**.'

'Thanks for being so worried about my dog with that ring inside her!' said Kyle. 'If we're all lucky you should get your *precious* ring back in a couple of days.'

'What do you mean?' I asked.

'When it comes out the other end,' said Kyle. 'But she does have **CONSTIPATION** problems, you know.'

I knew all about Francine's constipation problems. The Prime Minister of New Zealand knew all about Francine's constipation problems.

'But I need it now!' I said.

Just then Francine gave a little **cough** and spat the ring out at my feet. She hadn't swallowed it after all.

I **grabbed** it up off the grass. It was covered in doggy **drool** but I didn't care. I wiped it on my T-shirt and put it back on my finger.

'Oh! Thank you, thank you, thank you,' I said.

'Yeah, well, thanks for the **ice cream**,' said Kyle. 'Come on Francine.' And they headed off.

I thought of those **clown** heads back at the **carnival**, turning back and forth. Jason, Jason, Jason . . .

When I got home, Mum said, 'Have you finished packing?' and 'There's a letter for you' and 'Have you got orange **ice cream** on your shirt again?'

A letter? For me? I thought only old people got letters.

When I looked at the envelope, I saw there were lots of different

addresses on it, all crossed out except the last one — my address. And then I saw printed in the top left-hand corner of the envelope that it came from Rudiments of Chess Limited.

Rudiments of Chess was the name of my favourite book, given to me by . . . my great uncle Bill. But this couldn't have come from him because he was, well, dead.

I quickly took the letter to my room and opened it. It was handwritten.

My dear Jason,

Yes, it's your Great Uncle Bill here. I thought you might have guessed from the Rudiments of Chess Limited clue on the outside of the envelope.

Now, you might be thinking, 'How can this be from Great Uncle Bill when he is, well, dead?' But I can assure you that when I wrote this, I was very much alive. I devised a way of sending this letter around the world many, many times so it would take a long time to get to you. This letter has been to, among other places, Punta Arenas, Timbuktu, Chiang Mai and Hamilton.

I hope you are mostly enjoying being a secret agent. I know it won't be easy all the time. Sometimes you will not want to be brave. Sometimes people will be mean to you or just won't understand what you are doing. Sometimes you will feel alone. Sometimes you will make mistakes.

Well, don't worry about any of that. All you need to do is keep on being you. And everything else you can just, as a famous philosopher once said, 'Shake It Off!'

Wait a minute. Was Great Uncle Bill talking about a Taylor Swift song? I think he was. The letter continued:

I am proud of you.

Love, Great Uncle Bill'
PS This letter will self-destruct in ten seconds. But only if you set it on fire. Which is probably not a good idea.

Great Uncle Bill was right. Setting his letter on **fire** was not a good idea. Besides, part of it was **wet** because a bit of water from my eye had fallen on it. So I took a photo of the letter to keep on my phone, and put it away in a drawer.

9

If you look at a map of Europe, you will see that England and France are **SEPARATED** by a narrow piece of sea called the English Channel. The channel is just a little bit wider than Cook Strait, the narrow piece of sea between the North and South islands of New Zealand. And, just like in

New Zealand, you can get from one side to the other by travelling on a **FERRY**. But there is

another cool way of getting from England to France: on a very fast train called the **EUROSTAR**, which travels through an underwater **TUNNEL**.

When my mum heard that we would be travelling through an underwater tunnel, she was excited because she thought we would be able to see fishes and **SHARKS** and **octopuses** and other undersea creatures, like you can when you walk through the glass tunnel at Kelly Tarlton's Sea Life Aquarium.

I explained to her that the Channel Tunnel (which is what it is called) isn't a glass tunnel along the bottom of the sea. It goes even deeper than that — through the **rock** that is under the bottom of the sea. This means that even though you are underneath all the water and fishes and **octopuses**, all you can see when you look out the window of the **EUROSTAR** is the

concrete wall of

the **TUNNEL**

rushing by at

160 kilometres per

hour.

By the time we were looking

at the concrete wall rushing by, my mum had

got over her disappointment at not being

able to view the creatures of the sea and was

googling 'Top 10 most *romantic* places in *Paris*'

on her phone.

My dad was reading his latest copy of *Old-Style Volkswagen Beetle Restorer* magazine.

I was bored.

'**Come on**,' said Agent Rātana. 'I'll show you the carriage with the café.'

Wait. I'm getting ahead of myself. Ten pages ago I was on a park bench with a melty orange chocolate-chip ice cream and now I am on a very **Fast** train under the sea.

Here are the **HiGHLiGHTS** of what happened in between:

We travelled from Wellington to Auckland on an **Airbus A320**, and from Auckland to London via Los Angeles on a Boeing 787 Dreamliner. I watched all three *Ironman* movies and ate four airline meals including most of one my mum didn't want.

Once I turned the **WRONG WAY** coming out of the plane toilet and ended up in Business Class. Agent Rātana found me there asking a **friendly** flight attendant if she could show me how the evacuation **SLIDES** worked, and took me back to my seat.

Agent Rātana had come along as our special tour guide as part of the family-holiday-to-*Paris* prize I had '**won**'.

My mum and dad recognised Agent Rātana as the *nice* woman from the Ministry of Government Departments, who had spoken at Great Uncle Bill's funeral.

Agent Rātana told them she had given up working for the Ministry of Government Departments to follow her **dream** of being a tour guide, and wasn't that a lovely coincidence?

Of course, it wasn't a *lovely* coincidence at all and Agent Rātana was not really a tour guide, just like she hadn't really been a carnival ride operator on page 22.

After our plane arrived in London, we went to a hotel. We had to stay AWAKE without falling asleep until night-time, so we wouldn't be jetlagged the next day.

I stayed awake by watching *Avengers: Infinity War* and *Avengers: Endgame* and ordering an **ice cream** sundae from room service twice.

In the morning, we caught a **BLACK CAB** at St Pancras Station to catch the **EUROSTAR** train. I called it St Pancreas until my mum explained that a pancreas was a gland in your body — not just your body, obviously, everyone's body — but it's not something they name **railway stations** after. Or saints.

If you're wondering why we didn't fly straight to *Paris*, so we didn't have to travel under the English Channel in a train, you're about to find out.

'I'll have a ***chocolate éclair*** if they've got one,' said my dad. He gave me what looked like a New Zealand five dollar note, except it said '5 Euro' and had different pictures and colours and no Sir Edmund Hillary on it, but apart from that it was exactly the same.

'You know "éclair" is a *French* word, right?' my dad went on, 'so it's only right I try the local food.'

I followed Agent Rātana towards the back of the train, going through **carriages** full of people until we got to the one with the café.

'**WAIT HERE**, I need to check something,' she said and kept going.

My dad was in *luck*. They did have chocolate éclairs. I didn't know how to say, 'Can I please have a chocolate éclair?' in *French*, so I waved at the man behind the counter and pointed at it.

Agent Rātana returned from wherever she had been just as the man handed me the *chocolate éclair* in a small brown paper bag. Then he said, 'Here you go, sunshine!' in an English accent. Obviously, we hadn't got near enough to France that I needed to speak *French*.

'WE'RE GOOD TO GO,' said Agent Rātana. 'Follow me.' Then she looked down at the paper bag and added, 'Can you put that somewhere?'

'**WAIT** — where are we going?' I asked.

Agent Rātana leaned in close, checked no one was listening and said, 'To **BURP**.' Then she headed for the back of the carriage.

This was very **CONFUSING**. I had never gone anywhere to burp before. The Prime Minister had talked about **BURPING** too. Obviously, I still had a lot to learn about being a **s e c r e t   a g e n t**. I stuffed the chocolate-éclair-filled, small, brown paper bag in the pocket on the back of my shorts and then followed her.

There was another **carriage** after the one with the café. The door to it was closed and a sign on it said: **'Personnes Autorisées Uniquement — Authorised Persons Only'**.

Agent Rātana pushed some **BUTTONS** on a keypad, the door slid open and we stepped through.

The door closed behind us. This was the last carriage on the *EUROSTAR* train. There was no one else in it.

'Why is there no one in this one?' I asked.

'Because everyone else is going to *Paris*,' said Agent Rātana. She turned a knob and pushed a button and there was a **WHOOSH!**

As I looked through the narrow front window of the carriage I could see the rest of the *EUROSTAR* pulling away. Whatever Agent Rātana had done had uncoupled it from our **carriage**, which was now slowly slowing down.

It rolled to a **stop** right beside a little door in the **TUNNEL** wall. We were way underground, under the sea.

'This is where we get off,' said Agent Rātana.

The little door in the tunnel wall opened, and Agent Rātana and I stepped out of the carriage and straight into a **NARROW** corridor.

'Where is this exactly ?' I asked.

'**BURP**,' said Agent Rātana.

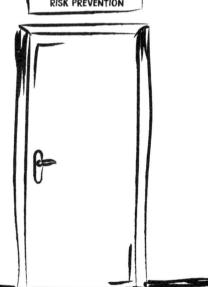

BUREAU OF UNDERCOVER
RISK PREVENTION

She didn't burp, she just said the word '**BURP**'.

At the end of the narrow corridor was another door. Above it was a sign that said **BUREAU OF UNDERCOVER RISK PREVENTION.**

I read it slowly:

'Bureau of Undercover Risk Prevention . . . BURP!'

Agent Rātana nodded. 'A **top-secret** international organisation that prevents EVIL baddies from carrying out their EVIL plans. And all top-secretly.'

'**Wow!**' I said. 'What's a bureau?'

'It's like an organisation or a department.'

'Why not call it the Department of Undercover Risk Prevention?'

'Because then it would be DURP,' said Agent Rātana. 'And DURP sounds silly. Come on, we don't want to keep BURP waiting.'

She pushed a **BUTTON** beside the door, it slid open, and in we went.

10

We walked into a big **OVAL** room. In the middle
of it was a big **OVAL** table with about
thirty high-backed black chairs around it.
The people sitting in the chairs all wore
SERIOUS-LOOKING suits and each
had a little national flag on the
table in front of them.

There was a person standing
up at the head of the table. It was
Colonel Croûton — the same *Colonel
Croûton* from page one of this book.

Except this was actually the first time I had seen her.

Agent Rātana looked very *impressed* by *Colonel Croûton*, and Agent Rātana didn't look very impressed very often.

'Colonel Michèle Croûton,' she whispered to me. 'Head of Security at **BURP**.'

On a huge screen behind *Colonel Croûton* was a giant map of *Paris* — which I recognised because it is a famous city, and also because the map had '*Paris*' written in the corner of it.

Agent Rātana pointed to two chairs just beside the door. As we slipped into them, two things happened.

First, I looked up to the ceiling and saw there wasn't any ceiling — just a glass dome, and above that was water . . . and fishes! We were on the sea floor! It was just like my mum had imagined the view from the train would be.

Second, as my **butt** settled into the chair, I felt a cream-filled chocolate éclair in a small paper bag being smooshed all over the inside of my back pocket.

'Watch and listen,' whispered Agent Rātana.

'Members of BURP,' said *Colonel Croûton*, 'as you will know, recently the EVIL mastermind Hugh Jarse was captured thanks to our friends in New Zealand.'

I looked at Agent Rātana. *Colonel Croûton* was talking about us!

'But now I have disturbing news about Hugh Jarse's longtime accomplice and sidekick, a woman who I am ashamed to say is *French*. Her name is Louise Papèr, although she calls herself Lou.'

Wait a minute... Hugh Jarse's longtime accomplice and sidekick was called Lou Papèr?

'**Shhh!**' said Agent Rātana. Oops! I had been thinking out loud again.

Colonel Croûton was still talking: 'If you want to know what Lou Papèr looks like, here she is . . .'

The screen filled with dozens of photos of faces. **DIFFERENT** faces — men and woman, young and old.

'We believe Lou Papèr has access to the very latest instant rubber face-mask technology,' said *Colonel Croûton*. 'She can make herself look like anyone, anytime. This is why she is called a master of **disguise**.'

'That's kind of cool,' I whispered to Agent Rātana, who moved her fingers across lips in a gesture that meant 'Zip it!'

Colonel Croûton continued: 'We can only be grateful that **Hugh Jarse** is behind bars in New Zealand. The last thing we need to see is **Hugh Jarse** and Lou Papèr together.'

I chortled.

Agent Rātana raised an eyebrow at me.

'But we still have a very **serious** situation on our hands,' *Colonel Croûton* continued. 'It seems that Lou Papèr has developed a new **WEAPON** —

a density-specific particle beam **disintegrator.** We know this because she sent us a video from a field in *Burgundy.*'

Playing on the big screen was a shaky video of a toilet bowl sitting in the middle of a field surrounded by some **clucking** chickens.

With a loud **ZZZZZAP**, the toilet bowl disappeared in a puff of white smoke!

Whoever was holding the camera ran up to where

the toilet had been. I could tell they were running because the picture went all **wobbly**.

When the wobbling stopped, the chickens were still there, *pecking* and **clucking**, but where the toilet bowl had been there was now just some white dust.

'This video proves that Lou Papèr's density-specific particle beam **disintegrator** works,' said *Colonel Croûton*. 'It can disintegrate any type of material you choose — and only that material. In this case . . .'

She stopped and looked at around at everyone in the room, then continued: '*Porcelain.* The substance that almost every toilet bowl in *Paris* is made from. Now, this brings me to Lou Papèr's **EVIL** plan, a copy of which has been obtained by some brave **BURP** agents.

The image on the screen changed to a close-up

of a handwritten note headed with the words 'Mon Plan Diabolique'.

Some people in the audience **GASPED**. Agent Rātana raised both eyebrows.

Colonel Croûton went on: 'Lou Papèr has attached a density-specific particle beam **disintegrator** to the radio mast at the very top of the Tour Eiffel. When switched on, the beam can reach and **DESTROY** any toilet bowl in the greater *Paris* area. She is planning on doing this at twelve o'clock midday tomorrow. One can imagine that the consequences for anyone sitting on the toilet at that time will not be very nice.'

Someone in the audience said '*Sacré bleu!*', which I think is *French* for 'Holy Moley!'

Someone with a German accent shouted, 'This must be stopped!'

'That will not be easy,' said *Colonel Croûton*. 'There's a clear view of the mast at the top of the Tour Eiffel from a three-hundred-and-sixty-degree angle. According to her plan, if Lou Papèr sees anyone trying to climb it she will immediately activate the **disintegrator**.'

Someone with an Italian accent said 'Mamma mia!' and someone else with an Australian accent said, **'Crikey dick!'** Then everybody started talking loudly at once.

Agent Rātana's phone **beeped**. She looked at it, said 'I have to take this,' and stepped out through the door.

Everyone around the table was still talking at each other despite *Colonel Croûton* saying **'QUIET PLEASE!'** and **'ATTENTION!'**

I shifted in my seat and felt the crushed **chocolate éclair** smoosh a little more. Checking no one was looking my way, I leant forward, pulled the **crumpled** paper bag out of my back pocket, put it on my knee and carefully **ripped** it open.

The **chocolate éclair** was not looking good. It was looking like it had been run over by a **STEAMROLLER**, or at least an eleven-year-old schoolboy's **butt**. The pastry was all cracked, and cream had **OOZED** out everywhere.

I had to get rid of it quickly before anyone noticed. If I crammed it into my mouth, licked the rest of the cream off the paper bag and squashed the paper bag up into a tiny ball and wedged it between the seats that might work. I made an executive decision.

And that is why, ten seconds later — when Agent Rātana returned from checking her phone and *Colonel Croûton* had calmed everyone down by telling them that the density-specific particle beam **disintegrator** could be deactivated thanks to the special skills of **Secret agent Jason Mason** from New Zealand, who was actually in the room right now, just over there — that was exactly when everyone else in the room turned and saw me with my mouth crammed full of **chocolate éclair** and cream smeared all over my face as I finished licking the paper bag.

'Just smile and wave,' Agent Rātana hissed.

I did as she said, and as I waved a small **blob** of cream flicked off the end of my finger and landed on her collar.

'I'd just like to apologise on behalf of the New Zealand government,' said Agent Rātana.

'It is nothing,' said *Colonel Croûton* as we were walking down another corridor away from the big oval room. 'I will clear up everything back there.'

'**That's great**,' I said, 'because I left a big blob of cream on the carpet.'

'I meant I will clear up any **misunderstandings** or concerns that the international members of BURP may have,' said *Colonel Croûton*. 'But the cream, yes, that as well.'

'Thank you so much,' said Agent Rātana, glaring at me.

We reached a lift at the end of the corridor and *Colonel Croûton* pushed the button to call it.

'You are very welcome,' she said. 'We are just so *grateful*, Jason, that you can use your secret power of ⓘⓝⓥⓘⓢⓘⓑⓛⓘⓛⓣⓨ to climb to the very top of the Tour Eiffel and deactivate the density-specific particle beam **disintegrator** without being seen.'

I gulped. *Colonel Croûton* hadn't actually explained that bit back in the **big** oval room. But I suppose it made sense.

I pointed back along the corridor and asked, 'Do they all . . .'

'Know about your s e c r e t power of ⓘⓝⓥⓘⓢⓘⓑⓛⓘⓛⓣⓨ? No. Only I do. I have special clearance from your prime minister. That is why it will

only be we three tomorrow at the top of the Tour
Eiffel.'

The lift doors opened with a **DING** and Agent
Rātana and I got out.

'Enjoy your evening in *Paris*,' said *Colonel
Croûton* as the lift doors closed.

'Well, she seems nice,' I said.

As we went up in the lift, Agent Rātana didn't
speak. I think she was cross at me because of the
chocolate éclair incident.

'Sorry about the **chocolate éclair** incident,'
I said.

'Hm,' said Agent Rātana.

It occurred to me that **Secret agent
Jason Mason** and the Chocolate Éclair
Incident would be a good title for a book, but I
decided not to say that out loud.

The lift had come out of the top of the underwater

81

headquarters of **BURP** and was moving straight up

a g̲l̲a̲s̲s̲ t̲u̲b̲e̲ heading for the surface of

the sea.

'I expected to see more fish,' I said.

No reply from Agent Rātana.

'Maybe they're on holiday.'

NOTHING.

'Do you know where fish go on holiday?'

There was a long pause, then Agent Rātana said,

'Where do fish go on holiday?'

'**Finland**,' I said. 'Fin-land. Get it? Because fish

have—'

'Yes, got it,' said Agent Rātana. She didn't **laugh**

but the corners of her mouth crinkled a little.

The lift *popped up* out of the sea next to a

helicopter landing pad, which was surrounded by

water. Sitting in the middle of the landing pad was

a **BURP** helicopter with its rotors spinning. You

could tell it was a **BURP** helicopter because it had '**BURP**' written in big purple letters on the side. The rest of the helicopter was painted in yellow, green and orange *swirls* — all the colours of my favourite flavour Fruit Bursts.

Agent Rātana and I ran over to it and climbed in the back door. As it took off I looked back and saw the helicopter pad **SINK** straight down until it disappeared under the water.

'I didn't expect a **top-secret** organisation's helicopter to look like this,' I said.

'No one expects a top-secret organisation's helicopter to look like this' said Agent Rātana.

'People look at it and think it's advertising **fizzy** drink. Sometimes the best place to hide is in plain sight. Now, let's get back on that train.'

I thought about telling Agent Rātana that the train was probably in *Paris* by now because in France it travels at 320 kilometres an hour. **(Fun fact:** that is more than three times the motorway speed limit in New Zealand.) But then I thought that **BURP** probably had that under control.

Sure enough, as we left the English Channel behind and crossed the coastline into France, I spotted the **EUROSTAR** sitting on the tracks in between some fields going exactly zero kilometres an hour.

The helicopter landed next to the last carriage (which was now the café carriage) and Agent Rātana and I got on at the back.

As we passed the man behind the café counter, he said, 'How was the **chocolate éclair**, sunshine?'

I remembered that my dad's **chocolate éclair** was now mostly in my stomach, but some bits of it were also on the floor of the secret headquarters of **BURP** and a few other places where I had wiped my hands when no one else was looking.

I realised that I would have to buy my dad a new **chocolate éclair** or give him his five Euros back — which I didn't have — to stop him from getting **SUSPICIOUS**.

In a whisper, I explained this all to Agent Rātana, who gave me one of her looks before getting out a five-Euro note and buying another éclair.

'That's the last one left,' said the man. '**LUCKY YOU**.'

'Lucky me,' said Agent Rātana.

Just then, the train began to move, and as we

made our way through the carriages, it quickly **SPED** up until the fields outside were *whizzing* past.

'There you are!' said my dad as we arrived back at our seats. 'I thought you must've got off and started walking. One of the ***fastest*** trains in the world, and we have to stop because the driver

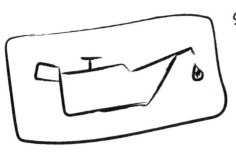

got an **ORANGE OIL LIGHT** on his dashboard. Technology! Did you get that ***chocolate éclair***?'

'Do you have chips?' asked my dad. 'Or do you call them *French* fries?'

My mum and dad and Agent Rātana and I were having dinner in a restaurant in *Paris*. And not just any restaurant. This restaurant was in the Eiffel Tower! Not in the little pointy bit up the top — that would be a tight squeeze — but in the **wider** bit about a third of the way up.

Agent Rātana had told my mum and dad that it was all part of the family holiday **prize**, but it was really a chance for her and me to do what Agent

Rātana calls a 'reconnaissance' and what I call 'checking the place out'.

'They don't call them *French* fries in France, Brian. That would be **silly**' said my mum. Then she said to the waiter, 'Un bol de chips, s'il vous plaît,' which (she explained to me) means 'a bowl of chips, please'.

While pretending to be our '**travel guide**', Agent Rātana suggested that tomorrow my mum and dad might want to visit the Palace of Versailles, a very big and expensive house built in the countryside by King Louis the fourteenth, which is famous for its gardens and ponds and fountains.

My mum said that would be *wonderful*, and my dad said he might get a few ideas for round the back of our place where he wanted to put in a deck and a **BARBECUE**.

Agent Rātana then suggested that while they were at Versailles she could take me to **Disneyland Paris. Disneyland Paris**! I'd never been to any Disneyland at all.

Lucy Johnson in my class has been to Disneyland Anaheim five times and Disney World Orlando twice, but her parents are rich.

Ricky Sugden said he'd been to Disneyland Texas and it's much **bigger** and better than Disneyland Anaheim.

Eric Chua said he didn't think there was a Disneyland Texas, but after Ricky gave him a **wedgie** he remembered that there was.

My mum and dad went over to the restaurant

window to take some **SELFiES** with _Paris_ in the background.

'Disneyland _Paris_ — yes!' I said.

'That's our **cover story**, right?' said Agent Rātana. Then, pointing straight up, she added, 'For when you're climbing this.'

Oh, right. For a second, in my excitement about meeting **Mickey Le Mouse**, I had forgotten about my mission.

'Actually, Jason, about your **MISSION** ...' said Agent Rātana.

UH-OH. Usually when an adult puts my name in the middle of a sentence like that it is followed by **bad news** (for example, about my goldfish or my great uncle Bill) or by the words 'I'm not **ANGRY**, I'm just disappointed'.

'There's been a change of plan,' Agent Rātana continued. 'It'll just be you and _Colonel Croûton_ on the **MISSION** tomorrow. I have to be somewhere else.'

'What? Where?' I said.

'I can't tell you,' she said. 'I don't even know myself'.

I must've looked confused because Agent Rātana looked like she was thinking about whether or not to tell me something, and then she looked like she had decided.

She *leant* in close. 'Flight Lieutenant Dan is in *Paris*, too. He's sent me a message inviting me on a **MYSTERY DATE** to somewhere *romantic* — at midday tomorrow.'

Luckily for her, I had finished eating all the chips from the bol de chips. If I hadn't, when I sat there with my mouth wide open it would have looked **gross**.

Flight Lieutenant Dan had helped out Agent Rātana and me by running across the field at an **ALL BLACKS** rugby match wearing only his undies (see my first book). I liked him. Agent Rātana liked him a lot. But I never thought she'd give up on a **MISSION** just to go on a date.

'I never thought you'd give up on a mission just to go on a date,' I said.

'I'm not giving up on a **MISSION**,' Agent Rātana said. 'It's your mission. You've got the special skills And you'll have *Colonel Croûton*. I've got to do this. This is *Paris* — the city of *romance!*'

Just then my mum and dad came back to the table.

'Well I'm ready for les **desserts**,' said my dad.

92

'What's *French* for 'pavlova'?'

That night, I had a bad dream about **climbing** the Eiffel Tower.

Here is a true fact: the tower is made of iron, and iron **expands** when it is heated up. So in summer when it's **HOTTER**, the Eiffel Tower expands and gets taller.

In real life it only gets taller by a few centimetres, but in my **dream** the day was so **HOT** that the tower just kept growing, and no matter how far I climbed I could never reach the top.

Luckily, I then found myself giving a speech to the school assembly in my pyjamas while sitting in a bathtub full of BAKED BEANS, which is how my dreams usually end. Then my school principal started SNORING.

I opened my eyes and realised the **SNORiNG** was coming from my dad. He and my mum and I were sharing a hotel room.

I looked out the window. The morning sun was **lighting up** the top of the Eiffel Tower.

'Remember Jason,' said *Colonel Croûton*, 'if
you fall from here, there will be no **SAFETY
ROPE**. There will be no bungee cord. There will
only be the small **emergency parachute** in
your backpack.'

If reading the above paragraph gives you a sense
of **DÉJÀ VU**, which is *French* for 'wait a minute,
haven't I been here before?', then don't worry.
Because here we are right back at page one, except
now you know how we got here.

While my mum and dad were at the Palace of

Versailles, and Agent Rātana was somewhere *romantic* with Flight Lieutenant Dan, I was about to climb up a skinny radio mast about as high as the top of the Auckland Sky Tower.

Luckily, I had *Colonel Croûton* with

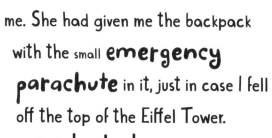

me. She had given me the backpack with the small **emergency parachute** in it, just in case I fell off the top of the Eiffel Tower.

As I **ducked** my head back down inside the hatch, she must have seen I looked a bit **scared**.

'Don't worry, Jason, you won't need it,' she said. 'For you, this job will be a piece of gâteau.'

I think she meant 'a piece of cake', which means 'SOMETHING EASY'. I have often wondered why that is, and which food item means 'something hard'. Maybe a **Gingernut**. That makes sense.

But at that moment, I wasn't thinking about biscuits.

'Remember, the density-specific particle beam disintegrator has a simple **ON–OFF** master switch,' said *Colonel Croûton*. I nodded. She had already shown me photos of it taken from B∪RP's not-so-secret-looking helicopter.

'You go invisible, you get outside, you climb up the mast, you switch the **disintegrator** off, you climb down the mast, you come back inside. If you do this while invisible then, as I say, a piece of gâteau.'

I nodded.

'But — and it is a very big but . . .'

When *Colonel Croûton* said 'very big but' I suddenly thought of **Hugh Jarse**. Focus, Jason, focus.

ON

OFF

'Remember,' *Colonel Croûton* continued, 'that somewhere, out there in *Paris*, she will be watching. And if you suddenly appear, she will activate the **disintegrator** and blow up every toilet bowl in the city. Never in history will so much mess have been made by Lou Papèr.'

I **gulped**.

'Okay,' said *Colonel Croûton* cheerily. 'Up you go!'

I took a **DEEP BREATH** and pushed the tiny button on my ring. My hands and arms and the rest of me disappeared. I had fifty-eight seconds.

'**Incroyable!**' gasped Colonel.

(I later googled the word 'incroyable' and it is *French* for 'incredible' or 'unbelievable'. I'd never been called '**incredible**' before, and I'd only been called 'unbelievable' when my teacher was talking about my **excuses** for not having done my homework.)

I **CLIMBED** the ladder out through the hatch, which was not as easy as it sounds because I could see the ladder but I couldn't see my hands and feet.

Soon though, I was standing on the outside of the not-quite-top of the Eiffel Tower.

I **looked** down. That was not a good idea. Way, way beneath me were tiny buildings and tinier cars and even tinier people. I put out an invisible hand, grabbed the narrow ladder on the radio mast and started **CLIMBING** again.

Apart from the whole invisibility thing, climbing a radio mast three hundred metres up in the air is not much different from being on the **JUNGLE**

GYM at school. Except if you fall off, of course.

Once I concentrated on the ladder in front of me, and not the view or the wind blowing around and up my shorts, climbing it was simple.

The density-specific particle beam disintegrator was only five or six rungs up the ladder. It was small — about the size of a bucket — and it was painted black. It had lots of **wires looping** in and out of it and had a big **ON-OFF** switch on the side of it. It was making a low humming sound.

All I had to do was turn the switch from **ON** to **OFF**, climb back down the ladder and get inside before fifty-eight seconds were up. Then I would have the rest of the afternoon free. Perhaps, as a reward, *Colonel Croûton* would show me the sights of *Paris*, by which I mean **Disneyland Paris**.

Holding tightly to the ladder with my left hand, I reached out my right hand and turned the switch off. The low **HUMMING** sound **stopped**. I had done it!

I quickly scrambled down the mast, shouting down through the hatch, 'I did it, *Colonel Croûton*! I turned it **OFF!**'

Colonel Croûton appeared just inside the hatch. When our eyes met, she had a strange look on her face.

'I know, Jason,' she said. 'Now give me the ring. And my name is Papèr. Lou Papèr.'

Have you ever noticed how time **SLOWS DOWN** sometimes? It never slows down when you are enjoying yourself. If I'm sitting enjoying one of my dad's creamed LAMINGTONS, time goes by very *Fast*. But if there is a plate of my dad's creamed lamingtons in the fridge for later, and I have

secretly taken one, then as I turn away from the fridge I trip and begin to fall, and I am trying to hold onto the LAMINGTON in my hand — and also hold onto the LAMINGTON in my other hand because I have actually taken two — that is when time slows down.

I have time in that moment to clearly think to myself that (a) this is probably going to **hurt**, and (b) this is definitely going to make a **mess**, and (c) I had better start thinking up an explanation. All of this happens in that **SPLIT-SECOND** before I **face plant** into one or, if I am unlucky, two creamed lamingtons.

The same thing was happening as my mind worked through what was going on. The goodie *Colonel Croûton* was in fact the baddie Lou Papèr. All of this had been part of her plan to get my invisibility ring. Also, I had about thirty-seconds of invisibility left.

'You have twenty-eight seconds of invisibility left. Give me the ring and I'll let you back inside,' said *Colonel Croûton*. . . I mean Lou Papèr.

I couldn't let that happen.

'**No!**' I shouted. 'I'll jump off and use the emergency parachute!'

'There is no emergency parachute,' she said. 'I lied. I'm the VILLAIN, remember? Fifteen seconds or the world finds out who you are!'

The world? I looked around. There was a helicopter HOVERING nearby. It had a TV camera poking out its side door, straight at where I was standing.

'Yes, I called the TV news,' said Lou Papèr. 'Get your best **smile** ready, not-so-Secret agent Jason Mason, or give me the ring. Seven seconds!'

At that moment, I would give anything to be back in my class learning about **hypotenuses**.

Suddenly, there was a roar, like the **ROAR** of a small jet-engine — or a JETPACK. A jetpack on the back of a person.

A figure in a **black jumpsuit** with a full-face black helmet suddenly *rose* up in the air right in front of me. They landed right beside me, then **kicked** the open hatch below us **SHUT**.

As the jetpack's roar died away, I could hear Lou Papèr shouting from under the hatch:

'Hé, que se passe-t-il?'*

[* translation: 'Hey, what's going on?']

The figure in black took one hand off the **JETPACK** controls, pulled a small canister off their belt and dropped it on top of the hatch. Purple smoke **billowed** up all around us. I couldn't see the TV news helicopter anymore. I guess that meant it couldn't see us either.

My invisibility was wearing off. I could see my hands, my feet, all of me.

The figure in **black** picked something else off their belt and gave to me, saying, '**QUICK**, put this on.'

It sprung open in my hand. It was a toy Ironman mask.

I adjusted the mask on my face as the figure in **black** spun me round one hundred and eighty degrees away from them. I could feel a **STRAP** going round my waist and two more under my arms, and I was pulled in tight in front of them. **Earmuffs** tightened around my ears, then suddenly the **JETPACK** fired up and we lifted off. **We were flying!** We cleared the purple smoke and *Paris* spread out all around, this time with no Eiffel Tower beneath me. Anyone who looked up into the sky would have seen a figure in a **black** jumpsuit and full **black** helmet wearing a **JETPACK**, and strapped to them someone who could have been a smaller version of Ironman if it wasn't for the **earmuffs** — and the T-shirt and shorts from Farmers.

We landed in a park (or as the *French* call it, un parc) near a street. A **black** van driving on the wrong side of the road pulled up and the side door slid open. The figure in black had already taken the **JETPACK** off and was carrying it to the van as they said, 'Come on, *QUICK!*' to me.

I jumped in, **CLICKED** in my seatbelt and took off the mask and earmuffs as the van drove away, still on the **WRONG** side of the road. But then I remembered that in France the wrong side of the road is the left side of the road, and we were on the right side of the road (which is the right side of the road).

The figure in **black** took off the helmet and said '**Kia ora, Jason**.' Of course she did. I had recognised that voice way back up at the top of the Eiffel Tower.

'Hey, Agent Rātana,' I said. 'Aren't you supposed to be with Flight Lieutenant Dan?'

'I am with Flight Lieutenant Dan,' said Agent Rātana. 'We're **rescuing** you.'

She looked to the front of the van. The driver turned round and gave me a NOD. 'Jason,' he said.

Flight Lieutenant Dan!

15

I had **questions** and I needed answers. Flight Lieutenant Dan was driving the black van along some streets in the middle of *Paris* while Agent Rātana and I sat in the back. I had learnt that the *French* word for street is '**rue**' and it goes at the beginning.

As I looked at the passing street signs I saw they had names like 'Rue Fabert' and '**Rue de Grenelle**'. I wondered if there

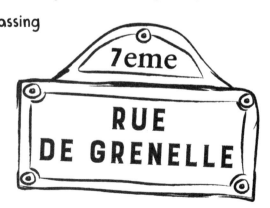

was a street called 'Rue de Words', but right now there were more important **questions** for me to ask.

'**Wait** — weren't you and Flight Lieutenant Dan going on a date somewhere *romantic?*' I asked in a low voice.

'**Of course not**,' said Agent Rātana, who seemed happy for Flight Lieutenant Dan to hear all this. 'That message I got inviting me on a date was **fake**. I knew it hadn't come from him.'

'It sure hadn't,' said Flight Lieutenant Dan from the front seat.

Agent Rātana continued, 'I knew that, because I know Flight Lieutenant Dan would never take me on a date to somewhere *"romantic".*'

When she said 'romantic', she **hooked** her index fingers up in the air like they were hanging up clothes on a washing line.

Well, this was just a bit **awkward**, I thought, but then Flight Lieutenant Dan said, 'Dead right I wouldn't. **Flowers?** Fancy meals? Beautiful sunsets? Forget it!'

Agent Rātana hadn't finished: 'And I would never want to go on a date with Flight Lieutenant Dan to somewhere *"romantic"* either,' she said.

'Me neither,' I said, trying to say something supportive.

Agent Rātana frowned at me and then said, 'But because I knew that message was **fake**, I knew someone was trying to separate me from your **MISSION** and **sabotage** it. Now we know that that someone was *Colonel Croûton* herself.'

'Or Lou Papèr,' I said.

'Lou Papèr,' Agent Rātana nodded. 'So I played along, pretended I was off with Flight Lieutenant Dan, when really I was preparing to pounce — like a **tiger**!'

'**ROWLLL**!' said Flight Lieutenant Dan.

'Well, thanks for saving me,' I said.

'Just part of the job, Agent,' said Agent Rātana.

Flight Lieutenant Dan turned the van into another rue. I leaned over to Agent Rātana and whispered, 'I thought you liked Flight Lieutenant Dan.'

'I do,' she whispered. 'That's why we're going to **Disneyland Paris** tomorrow.'

Disneyland Paris! Yes!

'That's so cool!' I said. 'Can I come?'

'No, Jason,' she said, patiently. 'It's a date.'

'Here we go,' said Flight Lieutenant Dan. 'The New Zealand Embassy.'

16

'Have a **Toffee Pop**,' said the New Zealand
Ambassador.

Agent Rātana and I were sitting in the
Ambassador's office in an important-looking old
building in the middle of *Paris*. The Ambassador
sat behind a big desk with a piece of green carved

pounamu and a laptop on
it. On the wall behind her was a
framed Silver Ferns uniform. On a
little table beside my chair was
a plate of **Toffee Pops**. It

would have been **impolite** not to take one, so I was extra polite and took two.

'You can call me Sharon,' said the Ambassador. 'I represent New Zealand.'

'What, in netball?' I said, looking puzzled at the uniform on the wall. I'm not saying Sharon was OLD, but I couldn't imagine her playing goal attack against Australia.

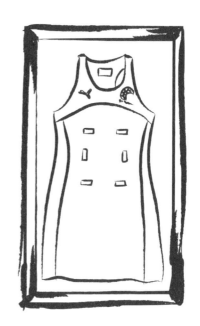

She smiled. 'No, no, I mean I represent the New Zealand government in France.'

She leaned towards us and, even though there was no one else in the room, added in a low voice '. . . and in BURP.'

I gasped. 'So, you were there the other day? Around the big table? Under the sea?'

Sharon the Ambassador nodded.

'I'm sorry about the **chocolate éclair**,' I said. 'I was just trying to get it all in my mouth and—'

'Jason, Jason, it's okay, it's nothing,' said Sharon. 'As it turns out, that was actually all tidied up by *Colonel Croûton* — or as we now know her, Lou Papèr.'

'Oh, well, that's one thing you can say,' I said. 'Lou Papèr is good for cleaning things up.'

I was **cracking** a joke, but as I looked from Sharon the Ambassador to Agent Rātana and back again, I saw that neither of them was **smiling**.

I should have **stopped** but I couldn't help myself.

'Yes,' I said, 'it would have been a sticky situation without Lou Papèr.'

There was no reaction.

'Yes indeed,' Sharon the Ambassador said, 'and

thanks to Agent Rātana here you are, safe. But that **EVIL** villain has disappeared.'

'You mean?' I said.

'Yes,' said **Sharon** the Ambassador. 'It turns out that Lou Papèr is very **slippery**.'

I quickly looked at Agent Rātana again and back to Sharon the Ambassador. No, that was not a joke.

'And as you yourself have discovered,' said Sharon the Ambassador, 'as a **MASTER OF DISGUISE**, she is especially skilled at being someone she isn't. She can change her look and she can change her *voice*. She can become any one of many different people, like an actor can take on many rolls.'

'You mean . . .?' I said.

'Yes,' said Sharon the Ambassador, 'the many **roles** of Lou Papèr.'

Lou Papèr. Many **rolls**.

Surely *that* was a joke. I checked again. **Nope.**

'But for the moment, anyway,' Sharon the Ambassador went on, 'Lou Papèr is out of our hands.'

I decided not to tell Sharon the Ambassador that she was really **wasting** some good **laugh** opportunities here.

Also, I had an idea that we hadn't seen the last of Lou Papèr. I bet you've had the same idea too. After all, we're only just past halfway in this book.

'By the way, Jason,' said Sharon the Ambassador, 'you should know that your great uncle Bill was very well thought of by the *French* government and **BURP**. He saved the day here during the **Whiffy Cheese** Emergency of 2017.'

The Whiffy Cheese Emergency of 2017? Something about that sounded familiar . . .

'I'm not sure I know about the **Whiffy Cheese** Emergency of 2017,' I said.

'Few people do,' said **Sharon** the Ambassador, 'thanks to your great uncle.'

A burst of music came out of Sharon the Ambassador's laptop. It was **Darth Vader's** theme song, the *Imperial March* from *Star Wars*.

DUM DUM DUM, DUM DE-DUM, DUM-DE-DUM

'A-ha,' she said, 'this is the top-secret video call I've been waiting for.' She pushed a button and said, '**PRIME MINISTER.**'

'Are they there?' said a familiar voice.

'Right here,' said **Sharon** the Ambassador, turning the laptop around so that Agent Rātana and I could see.

'Prime Minister,' Agent Rātana said.

'Agent Rātana,' the Prime Minister said.

'Is that a **dressing gown?**' I said.

'Yes, it is a dressing gown,' said the Prime Minister, who was wearing a dark purple dressing gown with 'PM' in *fancy* letters on the pocket. 'It's the middle of the night here. I just wanted to **CHECK** that you two were safe and also to say that I'm sure that won't be the last we see of Lou Papèr.'

See? Just as I told you, right?

'And, Jason, one more thing.'

Hmm, there was an adult using my name in the middle of a sentence again.

The Prime Minister continued: 'When you get back from your "**family holiday**" you and I will have a little chat.'

A little **chat**. That sounded nice, right? Out of the corner of my eye I could see Agent Rātana FROWNING at me.

'Right, that's all,' said the Prime Minister. 'Time for a warm cup of Milo and **beddy-byes**. Bonne nuit, as they say in France.'

'Bonne nuit, Prime Minister,' said Sharon the Ambassador, but the laptop screen had already gone blank.

'Well,' she continued, 'don't let rest of those **Toffee Pops** go to waste.'

And I didn't.

17

The last few days of our family holiday in France went by very **QUICKLY**. My mum and dad still had lots of sightseeing to do, and my mum had to buy **souvenirs** for my nana and aunts and uncles and cousins. She ended getting lots of tiny Eiffel Towers, and one for me too.

'So you'll always remember it,' she said.

I had a **feeling** I wouldn't be forgetting the Eiffel Tower any time soon.

I also got to see the most **FAMOUS** painting in the world at The Louvre. It is called the *Mona*

Lisa by **LEONARDO DA VINCI**, and it's a picture of a woman sitting with a kind of **weird** half-smile on her face.

Agent Rātana, who was still **acting** as our tour guide, told us that for hundreds of years no one has been able to figure out what the Mona Lisa's **half-smile** is about.

To me, it looked like, while **LEONARDO DA VINCI** was painting her, he'd been telling her about a friend of his with a name like Lou Papèr, and Mona was trying to keep a straight face. I knew that feeling well.

When we got on the plane to leave *Paris*, my mum and dad said they had had a great holiday.

This made me **feel good** because I know they do lots of things for me, even though that's their job and they have to do it **LEGALLY**, and also because sometimes I can be what one of my teachers once called 'a bit of a **handful**'.

My mum said that my great uncle Bill would have loved *Paris* and had always talked about wanting to visit. I didn't tell her that he had been here while he was working for **BURP** during the **Whiffy Cheese** Emergency of 2017, which still sounded **strangely** familiar.

My dad said he was really stoked to finally go with my mum on their honeymoon to the *City of Love*, and also that he had picked up some good ideas for the backyard barbecue area.

'I'll have to get **bitten** on the bum by a *meerkat* more often,' he said.

We arrived home at 11 o'clock on a Sunday night, and a new term of school was starting the next day. I was **jetlagged**, which has something to do with your body trying to adjust to different time zones. But to me just felt like I had been playing video games and drinking **sugary drinks** all night.

The next morning, I got to my classroom just as the bell **RANG**. Trying to keep my eyes open, I slid into my seat beside Kyle.

Before I could say anything more than '**Hey,**' our teacher Ms Dawson welcomed us back and asked who would like to tell the class what they did in the holidays.

Stacey Noovao told the class about learning netball skills. Zach Taylor told the class about performing in a **kapa haka** competition.

Ricky Sugden told the class about going **pig-hunting** with his uncle.

After a while Ms Dawson said, 'Let's hear from someone else now', and Ricky complained that he was just getting to the **interesting** bit.

Lucy Johnson would have told the class all about her holiday with her family in *Fiji*, but she was still on holiday with her family in *Fiji*.

'How about your exciting holiday in France, Jason?' Ms Dawson said.

As you know, Ms Dawson is also a secret agent, so she knew very well that it **hadn't** been just a holiday. But everyone knew I had been to France because of the competition on *Cruisy FM* with the Breakfast Zoo Morning Team.

'Yeah, **Mason**, what did you bring back for us?' said Ricky Sugden.

I **actually** had brought something back for everyone.

Right beside our hotel was a little **CHOCOLATIER**, which sounds like something you eat but is actually a shop that sells chocolates and lollies. The man behind the counter didn't speak English or call me '**sunshine**', but with some pointing, I managed to buy a big box of **NOUGAT**.

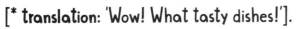

When I showed the **NOUGAT** to my dad, he said 'Oh là là! Quel plats savoureux!'

[* translation: 'Wow! What tasty dishes!'].

NOUGAT is a **chewy** sweet made out of egg whites, honey and nuts, and the sort I'd bought had rose petals, nuts and honey on the outside. There were enough pieces for the whole class.

Except when we got off the plane in Auckland, I found out that we were not allowed to bring the **NOUGAT** into New Zealand or we could be fined thousands of dollars! The honey and rose petals were a '**biohazard**'.

I thought a biohazard was like the **RADIOACTIVE** spider that bit Peter Parker, not some *French* lollies, but I had to get rid of them anyway.

I explained all this to my mum and dad, who were quite **tired** from flying halfway around the world. My mum pointed to the **big bins** that you could **dump** food into. My dad agreed, then suggested maybe we could get rid of some of the **NOUGAT** another way. He and I ended up eating about five pieces each.

All this meant that, when Ricky Sugden asked, 'What did you bring for us?', all I got out was, 'Well, nothing because—' before the whole class started groaning.

That was all they ended up hearing about my holiday in *Paris* because while Ms Dawson was saying **'Settle!'**, Agent Rātana came in, pretending to be a student teacher.

She whispered in Ms Dawson's ear and Ms Dawson said, 'Jason and Kyle, can you go to the principal's office please?'

The class went, **'Oooooh!'**.

Suddenly, I was wide awake.

'What's this about?' asked Kyle as we followed 'student teacher' Rātana down the corridor.

I wasn't exactly sure, but all of a sudden my mind flashed back to when the Prime Minister had said we would have to have a 'LITTLE CHAT'. Anyway, there wasn't much point in trying to explain. Kyle was going to find out for himself very soon.

'Things are about to get weird,' I said.

Sure enough, we didn't go to the principal's office. Instead, Agent Rātana and Kyle and I went out the back of the classroom block, through the little gate,

across the little bridge into the reserve and onto a Royal New Zealand Air Force NH90 medium utility helicopter.

With its big rotor blades going **THWOCK-THWOCK-THWOCK**, it took off and flew us across Wellington then landed on the roof of the *Beehive*.

There, Major Flatly — who was no longer wearing a **clown** outfit — met us and led us inside, past the signs marked "STEAM' and '*Water*' and 'EXTREME CAUTION: RADIOACTIVE BIOHAZARD'

and down the stairs to the big office with the amazing view.

He told us to sit on the sofa. So we did. Major Flatly and Agent Rātana kept standing.

'Don't sit on the **SPINNY** chair,' I said to Kyle, whose eyes had been sticking out like **ping-pong balls** ever since he'd first seen the helicopter.

The spinny chair **spun** round to reveal the Prime Minister, who said 'Good advice.'

Kyle **gasped**.

'Ah, Jason,' the Prime Minister said, looking me straight in the eye before turning and looking Kyle straight in the eye.

'Kyle, welcome. I'm the Prime Minister of New Zealand. That really was me with Jason on top of the **TOWER OF TREMBLES**. And everything you heard was true. Jason's Great Uncle

Bill. Jason's power of invisibility. Jason being a **secret agent**. All that stuff.'

Kyle just sat there with the sort of look on his face that my dad would call a **stunned mullet**'.

This was **GREAT NEWS!** The Prime Minister obviously thought that Kyle should know my big secret too! Although . . .

'Wait!' I said. 'How do you know that Kyle knows this?'

'Jason, Jason, Jason,' said the Prime Minister. 'I have **ears** everywhere.'

'Big **clown** ears?' I said, hoping for a friendly smile.

The Prime Minister turned back to Kyle and said, 'I know this is quite a lot to take in. Do you have any **questions**, anything you want to ask or say?'

Well, if I was Kyle, right then my top question would probably be: 'What did I eat just before going to bed because right now it's giving me the **weirdest** dream I ever had?' But he didn't. He just looked at me and said, 'I'm so sorry for not believing you.'

What a guy! What a friend! What a mate! Who would think to say something like that?

(Actually, Kyle later told me that he had really thought that he was having some crazy dream, like I had when I first heard all of this stuff, but he thought he would just — in his words — 'go with the flow'.)

'That's **okay**, Kyle,' I said. 'It's a lot to get your head around.'

Kyle thought for a second and then said, 'So . . . when we were at the **KIWI 1** rocket launch with Captain Burke Steel and his dog **Pixie**—'

There was a cough from the Prime Minister's direction, followed by, 'If I could just hurry you two along because I do have a country to run — with new and **IMPORTANT MISSIONS** . . . for the right people.'

Kyle and I looked at each other. Did this mean we would be working . . . together? Best mates on an exciting s e c r e t adventure with **thrills**, spills, hijinks, laughs and capers?

'So,' said the Prime Minister, 'hands up who wants to go on a new and **IMPORTANT MISSION**? Not so fast, Jason.'

'Sorry?' I said.

'It's a little late for sorry,' said the Prime Minister. 'You should've thought of that when you were telling Kyle here all that s e c r e t information. Secret government information. Secret government information that you *promised* not to tell anyone.

And yet you did. You broke the rules. **Spilled** the beans. Let the **cat** out of the bag.'

Oh, boy. Suddenly, I had a picture **flash** into my mind: Back when I was arguing with Kyle in front of those plastic **clowns** turning their heads back and forth. Except there was someone else there lurking in the background — the carnival ride attendant from the **TOWER OF TREMBLES**, the one who had said, 'Kid, you need to get on,' and who wasn't really a carnival ride operator at all. She must have heard Kyle and I **arguing**. She must have reported it back to the Prime Minister!

I thought again of the plastic **clowns** slowly shaking their heads. Except the last one wasn't a **clown**. It was my great uncle Bill, with a disappointed look on his face: 'Jason, Jason, Jason ...'

'So,' said the Prime Minister, interrupting my thoughts.

'If I can just **interrupt**,' said Kyle.

'Yes?' said the Prime Minister, with the look of someone who never gets interrupted.

'**Actually**, technically it wasn't Jason who said all of those things at the top of the **TOWER OF TREMBLES**. It was you. You **BROKE** the rules. **Spilled** the cat. Let the beans out of the **bag**. Technically.'

Kyle, you absolute legend!

The Prime Minister nodded slowly and then said, 'Technically, you say. Tell me Kyle, have you ever thought of becoming a lawyer?'

'No,' said Kyle.

'**Good**. Now, here's the thing, Kyle. This little meeting never happened. As far as anyone else knows the **official** story is that right now you've been called to the principal's office because your pet **poodle** Francine is . . .' (the Prime Minister checked some notes) '. . . suffering another **CONSTIPATION** event'.

'That's not very believable,' said Kyle.

'It's more **BELiEVABLE** than you getting on an Air Force helicopter to see the Prime Minister,' said the Prime Minister.

I put my hand up and said, '**Excuse me**, I'm confused.'

The Prime Minister leaned forward and said, 'Gentlemen, you two are the best of friends, are you not? And sooner or later, you, Kyle, were bound to wonder if maybe your good friend **Jason** was telling you the truth after all. So I'm just telling you, Kyle, **straight up**, that if you ever mention any of what you've learned to anybody then (one) they will not believe you and (two) you will be in a great deal of trouble indeed. **Are we clear?'**

Kyle's voice **squeaked** a little as he said, 'We're clear.'

'**Excellent**,' said the Prime Minister, leaning back in the **SPINNY** chair.

There was pause and then Kyle said, 'Is Jason in a great deal of trouble indeed?'

'Normally, he would be, yes. But Jason has done **IMPORTANT** vital work for the people of New Zealand. Vital work. So this time he gets a free pass.'

The Prime Minister turned to me and said, 'That will be all, Jason. You are **DISMISSED**. You are no longer required. Perhaps there'll be another **secret agent** mission one day. In the meantime, your licence to use your power of invisibility is hereby *REVOKED*.'

'Re— what? I said.

'Revoked' said Kyle helpfully. 'It means you're not allowed to go invisible'.

'Exactly, Kyle. Now, gentlemen, Agent Rātana will take you back to your classroom. I understand you're about to start learning about herbivores. **Exciting stuff**. Good luck with that.'

'But what about Lou Papèr?' I said. 'She could be anywhere.'

'Major Flatly here can handle Lou Papèr,' said the Prime Minister. 'Oh, and one more thing. When you two do get back to class, it's probably best that you're s e p a r a t e d. Jason, you can sit up the front by Lucy Johnson. I'm sure she'll have lots of **interesting** stories to tell you when she gets back from Fiji.'

I said 'But' again, then caught a look from Agent Rātana. I didn't say anything more, and Kyle and I got up and followed her out.

No one spoke on the **HELICOPTER** ride back to the little reserve behind Beardsmore Normal School.

When 'student teacher' Rātana took us back to the classroom, Ms Dawson said 'Ah, Jason, you'll be sitting up here now, by Lucy.'

'Oooooh!' said the rest of the class.

19

After school, I bought a packet of Cameo Crèmes at the service station and went round to the Twilight Views Rest Home and Villas to see my nana. I was glad she had moved to Wellington. But I always used to enjoy visiting her in Dunedin when I was small.

She would give me some home-made shortbread and ask me to help her with her crosswords and JiGSAW puzzles, and sometimes she said odd things. It always felt good seeing her, and I could do with feeling that way now.

I showed my nana some photos from *Paris* that were not part of my **secret agent MISSION**. She pulled a face when I showed her my photo of the Mona Lisa.

'Never trust someone who smiles like that,' she said. 'She's **HIDING** something.'

Then she said, 'You know, your great uncle Bill always used to come and visit me.'

'Well, he was your brother,' I said.

'Yes, my little brother,' she said, 'but he was so busy. You know, all that **being-a-secret-agent** business.'

I had just bitten off half of a Cameo Crème. I **CHEWED** and swallowed it as quickly as I could then blurted out, 'Sorry Nana, what was that?'

My nana looked this way and that, as if she was checking there wasn't a **foreign spy** hiding in

her ensuite bathroom or crouching down behind her **geraniums**. 'I can tell you now because I won't get him into trouble. But your uncle was a **secret agent** for the New Zealand government. And some other outfit too. What was it called? **COUGH? SNEEZE?**'

'**BURP?**' I suggested.

'That's it,' said my nana. '**BURP**. Good guess. What a silly name. They might as well have called it **FART**.'

'Just getting back to the **secret agent** business, Nana,' I said. 'Why exactly do you think he was one of those?'

'Because he told me, of course!'

I was about to put the second half of the

Cameo Crème in my mouth but decided not to. This needed my full attention.

'He told me,' my nana went on, 'a few years ago. After I had moved into *Shady Acres*. Ooh, the adventures he had! The Banana Skin Plot. The Disappearing Harbour Bridge. The Great Glue Flood. The Te Papa Painting **Heist**. And, of course, the **Whiffy Cheese** Emergency of 2017. Jason, you've dropped your biscuit.'

She was right. I had **dropped** my biscuit. I bet if you'd just heard this from your nana you'd have dropped your biscuit too.

'**Sorry**,' I said, picking it up. 'That sounds amazing. Just one thing — if this was all t o p s e c r e t, why did Great Uncle Bill tell you?'

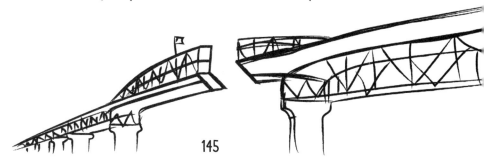

My nana took a big slurp of tea, looked thoughtful then said, 'I think he just needed to tell someone, so he told his big sister. We were always **best mates**, you know.'

She looked out the window for a bit. Then she took another **slurp** of tea and said, 'I imagine he thought it was quite safe to tell me. I mean, who would expect a **silly old lady** in a rest home to know top government secrets? And no one's ever come round asking me questions. Although Ken the podiatrist at *Shady Acres* who used to do my feet was always a bit nosy.'

'You're not **silly**, Nana,' I said.

'Good answer, **Jason**,' she said. 'Mind you, your great uncle Bill was very naughty, wasn't he? He promised not to tell something important to anyone and then he did. He **broke** his promise.'

Well, this was **embarrassing**. I had done

exactly the same with Kyle, as the Prime Minister
of New Zealand had pointed out, and here was my
own nana reminding me (even though she didn't know
about it). My **cheeks** felt very **HOT**, like you
could fry an egg on each side of my face.

'Still,' my nana said, 'nobody's perfect, are they?
Not even Bill. And that's good. People would be very
annoying if they were **perfect**. That's why I make
a habit of doing one ᴺᵃᵘᵍʰᵗʸ thing a day.'

She must have seen me **frown** because she
added, 'Don't worry, I've already done today's one. It
involves Mrs Wilson at number

32 and a **frog**,
which was not hurt.
No harm done,
that's the thing. Same
with Bill telling me
things he shouldn't have.

As I always say, at the end of the day no one's going to lose their TROUSERS.'

My nana did always say that, and other things like it.

Kyle and I had once made a list of the strange sayings my nana had told us. We got up to thirty-seven.

Right now though, my head was SPINNING with the other things my nana had said, so I told her I had to go and do my homework (which was not untrue, because I had to catch up on herbivores which, it turned out, were not as exciting as the Prime Minister had said).

At the door, I gave my nana a *kiss* and she said, 'That Bill, you know, sometimes I was a bit jealous of all those **adventures** he got to go on. Now, bring me another packet of those biscuits next time and I'll tell you all about his power of invisibility.'

He had told her all about his power of invisibility! Naughty old Great Uncle Bill, I thought. No. Good old Great Old Uncle Bill.

At the same time, another thought (that I didn't even know I was thinking yet) started forming way in the back of my **brain**.

I walked back towards my house, mulling over what my nana had just told me. '**Mulling**' means 'thinking', but it sounded better for what I was doing right then. I needed a good mull.

From behind me, I heard a familiar musical tune — the sound of an **ice-cream** van.

Not just any ice-cream van, but Agent Rātana's special **undercover** one. It pulled up beside me and I got in.

Agent Rātana handed me a *bright* orange wig and said, 'Put this on. And your seatbelt too.'

'What's this for?' I asked, putting on the wig. 'Who am I supposed to be, Ed Sheeran's little brother?'

'Just as long as you don't look like **Jason Mason**,' said Agent Rātana, as she pulled out into traffic, still with the '**come and get your ice creams**' music blaring. 'I'm not supposed to be speaking with you. Prime Minister's orders.'

'Are you **MAD** at me like the Prime Minister?' I asked.

'We haven't got time for that,' she said. 'I think Lou Papèr is on the loose.'

'On the **LOO**?' I said.

'No, on the **LOOSE**,' she said. 'Right here in New Zealand.'

Through the window, I could see a man on a

bike pedalling very fast in an effort to keep up with us while making **ice-cream-licking gestures** with one hand. It looked like he wanted us to sell him one.

'Can you stop that music?' said Agent Rātana.

I'd done this before. I **hit** the button on the dashboard in just the right way. The 'come and get your ice creams' music slowly wound down, like the sound of someone finishing playing the **bagpipes**.

Agent Rātana sped up and, in the side mirror, I saw the man on the bike change from making **ice-cream-licking gestures** at us to some other gestures, which were quite **RUDE**, before losing control and **wobbling** into a hedge on the side of the road.

'Lou Papèr on the loose,' I said. 'Does the Prime Minister know?'

Agent Rātana shook her head.

'The Prime Minister only listens to what Major Flatly says,' she said, 'and Major Flatly says it's **impossible** for Lou Papèr to get into the country. He says every airport, seaport, heliport and SPACEPORT is being checked. He says the Police, the Army, the Navy, the Air Force, the Diplomatic Protection Squad, the Dog Squad, the SAS, the SIS and the Coastguard have it all under control.'

'Does he know that Lou Papèr is a master of disguise?' I asked.

Agent Rātana gave me a look that said, 'I know, right?' and passed me her phone.

'So anyway, yesterday Flight Lieutenant Dan and I went to the *Museum Of Olden-Day Things*.'

'On another date?' I asked.

'That's not the point,' said Agent Rātana. 'There

was an exhibition of medieval siege weapons that we were both very interested in.'

She handed me her phone. There was a photo on it — a selfie of her and Flight Lieutenant Dan in front of something that looked like a giant catapult.

'A **trebuchet**. Cool,' I said. 'Do you know they used to attack castles with these things by using them to throw **dead pigs** with diseases over the walls?'

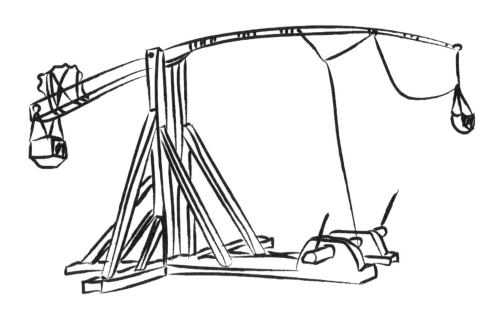

I could tell that Agent Rātana was, in fact, very interested in this fact and may have liked to know more, but all she said was, '**SCROLL DOWN**.'

The next photo was of a full suit of **armour**, like a knight would wear.

'That's a full suit of armour, like a **knight** would wear,' I said.

'Correct,' said Agent Rātana. 'This one was part of a special exhibit at the *Museum Of Olden-Day Things*. It had just arrived . . . from France.'

France. **Hmm.** A suit of armour. **Hmm.** You could fit a person inside a suit of **armour**. After all, that's what they were for. You could hide in one all the way to New Zealand from France. You'd have to keep very still though. But that wouldn't be **impossible** if you were . . . a master of disguise.

'Exactly!' said Agent Rātana. I had been thinking out **loud** again.

Agent Rātana went on to describe strange goings-on that had been going on at the *Museum Of Olden-Day Things*. She told me that she and Flight Lieutenant Dan had been the last to leave the museum at closing time as they had been looking at a scale model of a **battering ram**.

(By the way, I have to say that between Disneyland *Paris* and the exhibition of medieval siege weapons, I was very impressed by the kind of dates that Agent Rātana and Flight Lieutenant Dan were going on. It certainly beat all that staring-into-each-other's-eyes stuff people do in the movies).

Just before closing time, when all the other visitors had left and Agent Rātana and Flight Lieutenant Dan were leaving too, they went past the suit of **armour**. Except the suit of armour wasn't standing up anymore. It was in BiTS AND PIECES all over the floor.

'I'm just saying,' Agent Rātana said to me, 'if there had been someone inside that suit of **armour**, they weren't there anymore.'

'Someone like Lou Papèr?' I said. 'Are you sure?'

Agent Rātana said 'It's just a hunch.'

'Well, you know what they say,' I said.

'**Hunches are like lunches**. You can't ignore them, or you'll get a bad feeling in your stomach later.'

That's not what they say, of course. That's not what anyone says. I was just trying to think up something supportive to say to Agent Rātana.

She **FROWNED** and said, 'If I tell Major Flatly and the Prime Minister, they'll just **laugh**. I don't know what to do.'

I thought for a bit, then said, 'We need more information, and I know where to find it — **Hugh Jarse**.'

Agent Rātana nodded, carefully checked the rear-vision mirror, flicked on the indicator and pulled the ice-cream van around in a **SCREECHING** U-turn.

Unlike the Twilight Views Rest Home and Villas where my nana lives, the **Stony Lonesome Corrections Facility** actually was a prison. It was a big, grey building with a big fence around it. There was a visitors' carpark out the front, and today was probably the first time ever that an **ice-cream** van had parked there.

Stony Lonesome Corrections Facility

'Follow my lead,' said Agent Rātana as we walked up to the entrance.

The glass doors slid open and Agent Rātana headed straight for a **big**, wide desk with a **big**, tall prison guard behind it.

She showed the guard something on her phone and said 'Rātana, Ministry of Government Departments, to see Jarse.'

The guard tapped at her computer and said, **'Security level . . . crimson.'** She raised her eyebrows — whatever a crimson security level was it must have been good, like a *BLACK BELT* in KARATE, which Agent Rātana probably also had.

Then the guard looked at me and said, 'What about him?'

Agent Rātana said, 'It's Bring Your **NEPHEW** to Work Day today.'

The guard **FROWNED** and said, 'There's no option on the computer for that.'

Agent Rātana held out her phone and said, 'Do you want to **explain** that to the Prime Minister?' (Of course, she didn't really have Prime Minister on the phone right then, but she hadn't said that she did. She'd just asked, 'Do you want to **explain** that to the Prime Minister?' I thought that was quite **clever**.)

The guard thought for a second, then she said, **'CLEARANCE APPROVED — THAT WAY,'** and we headed the way she had pointed.

As we walked away, I said, 'This is so exciting, *Auntie*,' loud enough for the guard behind us to hear.

We had to go through a metal detector, which weirdly didn't get set off by Great Uncle Bill's ring, but did get off by my asthma inhaler.

Then we walked along a corridor under a sign that read '**D BLOCK: ARCH-VILLAINS AND NOTORIOUS CRIMINAL MASTERMINDS**' and along to another desk with lots of screens and buttons.

D BLOCK

ARCH-VILLAINS AND NOTORIOUS CRIMINAL MASTERMINDS

Sitting at the desk was a guard called **Nobby**. I knew he was called Nobby because Agent Rātana said, '**Kia ora Nobby**, this is Jason.'

It seemed that this was not the first time she had been here visiting an arch-villain and/or notorious criminal mastermind.

Nobby said, 'Hi Agent Rātana. Hello Jason.'

He looked at his computer, and said, 'I'll just check that **Hugh Jarse** hasn't popped out. That wouldn't be a good look! **Ha! Jokes**. No, he's there of course. Around the corner and right down the end.'

As we turned the corner, I looked down another corridor. Down at the end, facing right at us, were the bars of a prison cell. As we got closer, through them I could see **Hugh Jarse** standing there looking right back at us.

'I'll try not to say anything that'll get us in **trouble**,' I said.

'Bit late for that,' said Agent Rātana. 'Don't get too close.'

We stopped at a distance of approximately two cubits from the bars of the prison cell.

(A cubit is an ancient unit of length based on the distance from the elbow to the tip of the middle

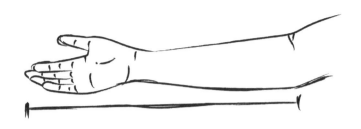

finger. I like **interesting units** of measurement and am trying to use them more in my writing. But that will have to wait for a **smidgeon**, because right now I was looking straight at arch-villain and criminal mastermind, **Hugh Jarse**.)

'Well, well, well, **Hugh Jarse**,' I said.

'That's Mister Jarse to you, **Secret agent Jason Mason**. Who are you supposed to be — Ed Sheeran's little brother?'

I had forgotten I was still wearing the orange wig. **Hugh Jarse** turned to Agent Rātana. 'And you, **Secret agent** Shirley Rātana.'

'You first name is Shirley?' I said out of the corner of my mouth to Agent Rātana.

'Not now,' she replied through gritted teeth.

Hugh Jarse laughed one of his 'A har har!' laughs and said, 'You'll be surprised what I know about both of you. How was your date at the museum with Flight Lieutenant Dan, Shirley?'

Agent Rātana **GASPED**.

'Now is there a reason for this visit?' **Hugh Jarse** continued. 'Because you're interrupting my escape plans. Lou Papèr will be here and I will be out of here before you can say pneumonoultramicroscopicsilicovolcanoconiosis.'

'Pneumonoultramicroscopicsilicovolcanoconiosis,' I said. 'The longest word in most English dictionaries.'

I knew that because I'd **memorised it** once when I should have been learning about the properties of integers.

'That's IMPOSSIBLE,' said Agent Rātana.

'No, it's **actually true**,' I said. 'It has forty-five letters, and it means—'

'**No, no**,' Agent Rātana said. 'I mean it's impossible for Lou Papèr to get in here.'

'I wouldn't be so sure, Shirley,' said **Hugh Jarse**. 'You'd be surprised the places Lou Papèr gets into. She's a MASTER OF DISGUISE — and there's nothing either of you can do to stop us.'

'You know what, **Mr Jarse**,' I said, 'I remember the first time I met you. At Eden Park. By the snack machine. You took the very last packet of **Twisties**. The packet I wanted. I knew right then you were a **BAD, BAD** man.'

'A HAR HAR HAR!' Hugh Jarse laughed his villainy laugh. I wondered if he practised it in front of the mirror.

'Ah yes', he said, 'and soon I will have all the packets of **Twisties** I want whenever I want them! Mmm . . . **Twisties**. Cheesy, orange-coloured corn snacks . . .'

'I've heard enough,' I said. 'Come on, Shirley.'

Agent Rātana and I turned and started walking away. As we did, she muttered under her breath, 'Just call me Agent Rātana, will you.'

Behind us, Hugh Jarse's laugh echoed along the corridor: 'A HAR HAR! A HAR HAR HAR!'

We turned a corner and stopped.

'I was right,' said Agent Rātana. 'That was Lou Papèr at the *Museum Of Olden-Day Things*. She's in the country and on the loose.'

'It's worse than that,' I said. 'You know how **Hugh Jarse** said Lou Papèr would get him out of here before I could say pneumonoultramicroscopicsilicovolcanoconiosis?

'Well, she didn't, did she,' said Agent Rātana.

'Yes, she did,' I replied.

Agent Rātana looked **puzzled**.

'Remember when I said to him about taking the last packet of **Twisties** from the machine?' I said.

'To be honest,' said Agent Rātana, 'I didn't think that was so bad. I've done it myself.'

'But they weren't **Twisties**,' I said. 'There never were any **Twisties**. I changed that bit in the story. At Eden Park, **Hugh Jarse** actually took the last packet of **BURGER RINGS**.

'Also an orange-coloured corn snack,' Agent Rātana pointed out.

'But not so CHEESY,' I replied. 'The real Hugh Jarse would have known the difference and remembered it. He would've pointed out my mistake just then when I said it.'

'You mean. . .'

'Yes. That person we were speaking to just then was not Hugh Jarse.'

22

'There,' said Nobby. '**Hugh Jarse**'s mother, Marge Jarse.'

We were back at **Nobby's** desk where Agent Rātana had asked Nobby if **Hugh Jarse** had had any visitors.

Nobby was pushing **BUTTONS** and pointing to a screen. It showed the corridor that Agent Rātana and I had just been walking down. An old, grey-haired lady wearing a cardigan, a skirt and a scarf over her head was walking beside

a **prison guard**.

'When did this happen?' asked Agent Rātana.

'Earlier this morning. She didn't stay for long,' said **Nobby**. 'Probably not much to talk about. You know, "Well, son, got any EVIL plans for the weekend?" "No, Mum, I'm in here, remember?" That sort of thing. Now if you look here . . .'

Nobby pushed some more **BUTTONS** and we saw the grey-haired lady with the cardigan and skirt and the scarf walking back the other way with the **prison guard**.

'See,' Nobby said. 'Here's Marge Jarse walking out again, ten minutes later.'

Agent Rātana and I looked at each other.

'I have a bad feeling about this,' I said.

'**Nobby**,' said Agent Rātana. 'We don't think that "old lady" was Marge Jarse, either going in or coming out. We think it was Lou Papèr coming in and **Hugh Jarse** going out.'

'Wait, what?' said Nobby.

'Lou Papèr,' I explained, 'is a master of disguise. She disguised herself as **Hugh Jarse**'s mum to get in to see him. Then she disguised **Hugh Jarse** as his mum, so he could escape. Then she stayed in his cell and disguised herself as **Hugh Jarse**, so no one would realise that the real **Hugh Jarse** had escaped.'

'Lou Papèr **can do all that?**' said Nobby.

'They do call her a master of disguise,' I said.

'No way! That sounds like a movie!' said **Nobby**.

It does sound like a **MOVIE**, and depending on how well this book sells it might one day actually be one. But it was also, I was pretty sure, true.

Nobby wasn't so certain. 'So you're telling me that right now Lou Papèr has replaced **Hugh**

Jarse in his cell? What's she supposed to do now?'

'Escape from it too, I think,' I said.

'I'm sorry,' said Nobby, 'I find this very whole story hard to believe. Anyway, Hugh Jarse had an appointment with Doctor Lurgy . . . right about now, in fact.'

'Doctor . . . Lurgy?' said Agent Rātana.

'The prison doctor. Hugh Jarse asked to see him. He said he had a nasty pimple in an embarrassing place.'

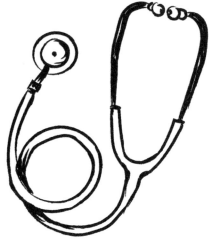

'Nobby,' said Agent Rātana in a calm voice that I knew meant something UNCALM was about to happen, 'can we see the live camera in the corridor please?'

'You betcha,' said Nobby. He pushed a

BUTTON, and on the screen we could see the corridor we had just been in. A man in a white doctor's coat with a stethoscope round his neck was leaving through a door marked '**EXIT THIS WAY**'.

'That's **Doctor Lurgy** now,' said Nobby. 'Obviously he's finished with **Hugh Jarse**'s pimple. He must be off on his lunch break.'

'**Yessss**,' said Agent Rātana. 'Can we also have a look at the live camera outside, at the entrance?'

'Coming right up,' said **Nobby** as he pushed another **BUTTON**.

Now we could see outside the front of the prison. **Doctor Lurgy**, in the white coat and stethoscope, walked out through the sliding glass doors into the visitors' carpark. There were no cars in the visitors' carpark, but there was Agent Rātana's **ice-cream** van. **Doctor Lurgy** walked right up to the driver's door and stopped.

'She's breaking into my **ice-cream** van!' said Agent Rātana.

'She?' said **Nobby**.

'That's not **Doctor Lurgy**. It's Lou Papèr — and she's breaking into my ice-cream van.'

'You have an ice-cream van?' said Noddy, puzzled.

'It's a long story,' I said.

'**SOUND THE ALARM!**' said Agent Rātana, not quite as calmly.

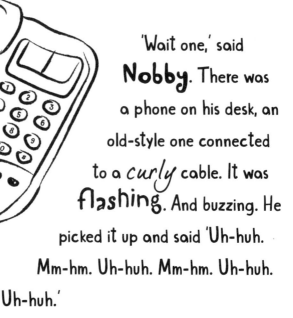

'Wait one,' said **Nobby**. There was a phone on his desk, an old-style one connected to a *curly* cable. It was **flashing**. And buzzing. He picked it up and said 'Uh-huh. Mm-hm. Uh-huh. Mm-hm. Uh-huh. Uh-huh.'

He put the phone down and turned to us. 'Well,' he said, 'they've just found the real **Doctor Lurgy** tied up in **Hugh Jarse**'s cell — without his white coat or stethoscope.'

'Because Lou Papèr is wearing his white coat and stethoscope,' said Agent Rātana. 'In my ice-cream van. Driving away right now! **SOUND. THE. ALARM!**'

'Just so I understand—' said **Nobby**.

There was a big red button marked **'GENERAL ALARM**' in the middle of **Nobby's** desk. Agent Rātana threw herself at it and **SLAMMED** the palm of her hand down on it.

All at once there was an **incredibly loud** noise of sirens and alarm bells going off, and red lights **flashed** from the ceiling.

'I was just about to do that,' said Nobby.

'We should chase her!' I said.

'What in?' Agent Rātana replied.

She pulled her phone out of her pocket. It was **buzzing**, and 'PM' was **flashing** on the screen. The alarm bells and sirens were still going off, so she had to hold the phone up to one ear, hold her hand over her other ear and talk quite **loudly**.

I don't know if you've ever tried to **figure out** what was going on in a phone conversation when you can only hear one person **speaking**, but this one went like this: 'Rātana here, Prime Minister... Yes, Hugh Jarse is on the run. And so is Lou Papèr ... No really, she is. She's in New Zealand and ... How do I know? Well, there was a suit of **armour** and an old lady who looked like Marge Jarse and ... No, Prime Minister, I can assure you I'm not **imagining** things, this is all true ... But—'

Agent Rātana was looking more and more down as her conversation with the Prime Minister went on. Then she said, 'Yes, I have been talking with

178

Jason Mason . . . Yes, I know you ordered me not to, but . . . Yes, he is, in fact, with me right now . . . Yes, here in the **prison** . . . Well, I told them it was Bring Your Nephew to Work-Day . . . No, it's not Bring Your Nephew to Work Day . . . No, he's not my nephew . . . Well, yes Prime Minister, *technically* I have **DISOBEYED** your orders but . . . but . . . but . . .

I understand Prime Minister. *Goodbye.*'

She put her phone back in her pocket.

I put on my **cheeriest face** and asked, 'How's the Prime Minister? Any news?'

Just then the **ALARM BELLS** and sirens stopped, so I could hear the next thing Agent Rātana said very clearly.

'I am also *DISMISSED*,' she said. 'And no longer required.'

'I used to come here every Thursday after school,'
I said.

Agent Rātana and I were sitting in the **ice-cream van**, parked outside where my great
uncle Bill's house used to be.

It turned out that Lou Papèr had not gone
very far in the ice-cream van she'd **STOLEN**. The
'come and get your ice creams' **MUSIC** had started
playing as soon as she'd driven off. That's not
something you want if you're on the run, even if you
are a **MASTER OF DISGUISE** dressed up as a doctor.

So Lou Papèr had left the ice-cream van on the side of the road, **waved** down a passing car and asked the driver if she could borrow it because she had to go and deliver a baby. That was the last anyone had seen of her.

Agent Rātana and I had found the **ice-cream van** soon after that, but we didn't know what to do next. We were 'no longer required'.

It was like being a **star try-scorer** on the school rugby team and then being taken off field by the coach and not even being trusted to hold the half-time oranges.

(**Note:** I have never actually been the star try-scorer on the school rugby team. My usual position is 'standing on the sideline eating a *banana*', but I have a good imagination).

I had given Agent Rātana directions to drive to where my great uncle Bill's house used to be. When we pulled up in the **ice-cream van**, I saw something new was being built there. It was some new shops. A sign said, 'FISH AND CHIPS — OPENING SOON!'

I felt a little better that one day I would be able to visit where my great uncle Bill had lived and order a fish, a hot dog and a SCOOP OF CHIPS. It would be a way of **honouring** his memory, and also **tasty**.

I could tell Agent Rātana was feeling low. She had been on a lot of missions with Great Uncle Bill.

'It's like I'm letting him down,' she said. She said it in the same way you would list groceries: '*Spaghetti* and sausages, toast bread, **dishwashing liquid**, it's like I'm letting him down.'

'I don't think he'd think that,' I said. 'He told me something once. Wait, I'll get it.'

I got out my phone, found the photo of Great Uncle Bill's letter, and read out some of it: 'Sometimes you will feel alone. Sometimes you will make MISTAKES. Well, don't worry about any of that. All you need to do is keep on being you. And everything else you can just, as a famous philosopher once said—'

Agent Rātana interrupted me. '**Shake It Off?**' she said, grinning.

'Yes!' I said. 'How did you know?'

'He told me the same thing,' she said. 'I did not expect the **Taylor Swift bit**.'

'Me neither,' I said. 'Maybe we should take his advice.'

Agent Rātana nodded slowly.

'**Okay**,' she said. 'Let's make a list.'

'What, like groceries?

'No, assets and liabilities. Things we've got going for us and things that are problems for us.'

I hadn't got to this bit of s e c r e t a g e n t training yet, but it sounded like a good idea. I use my phone to make our list. Here it is:

ASSETS

One ice-cream van

(that's all we could think of)

LIABILITIES

No help from the Prime Minister, who is cross with us

No help from Major Flatly, who doesn't believe us

No help from the Police, the Army, the Navy, the Air Force, the Diplomatic Protection Squad, the Dog Squad, the SAS, the SIS, or the Coastguard (see above)

No jetpack (Agent Rātana had borrowed it from BURP in Paris and had given it back)

No idea where notorious criminal Lou Papèr was or what her evil plans were

No idea where notorious criminal Hugh Jarse was or what his evil plans were

'That's some list,' said Agent Rātana.

Right then my phone lit up with a video call. It was from an unknown number but I took it anyway. The screen changed to a smirking face I knew only too well.

'**Hugh Jarse**,' I said.

'Hello **Jason Mason**,' he said. 'And before you ask, yes, I am the real **Hugh Jarse**. Lou Papèr tells me you came to visit me in prison. Sorry I missed you, but as you now know I had indeed escaped before you could say pneumonoultramicroscopicsilicovolcanoconiosis.'

'Where are you?' I said. 'What are you up to? What are you planning?'

'What is this, some kind of QUIZ SHOW?' said **Hugh Jarse**. 'As it happens I'm in the EVIL genius workshop at my EVIL genius headquarters. The rest you'll find out at eight-thirty tonight at the TOWER OF TREMBLES.'

The **TOWER OF TREMBLES**!

'The **TOWER OF TREMBLES**?' I
gasped.

'Yes, the **TOWER OF TREMBLES**. Is
there an echo in here? Be at the **TOWER OF
TREMBLES** at eight-thirty tonight . . . or else!'

'Or else what?'

'That is all. Toodle-oo!' said Hugh
Jarse.

'Wait!' I said. But he had gone. At least this meant
I could delete the last thing from our list.

'What does he want at the **TOWER OF
TREMBLES**?' said Agent Rātana?

'I think he has Lou Papèr's density-specific
particle beam disintegrator.'

Agent Rātana gave me a 'why do you think that?'
look and I showed her my phone.

I had taken a screen shot of Hugh

Jarse in his **EVIL** genius workshop. There, right behind him, was a **black object** about the size of a bucket, with lots of wires looping in and out of it and a big '**ON-OFF**' switch.

Agent Rātana nodded.

'If I'm right, this is just like *Paris*. Except this time **Hugh Jarse** and Lou Papèr are working together, we have no help, and if they succeed every toilet bowl right here in Wellington will be **disintegrated**,' I said.

'Are you sure?' asked Agent Rātana.

'It's just a hunch,' I said.

'Well, you know what they say,' she said. '**Hunches are like lunches.** We'd better stop them.'

I smiled. Agent Rātana was back in the game!

'I agree,' I said. 'All we need is a plan.'

'Do we have a plan?' she asked.

'I have half a plan,' I said, 'but I'll need to talk to someone.'

I got out my phone and started messaging Kyle.

24

It was 8.25pm. The sun had gone down and the carnival, which was closed for the night, was in darkness.

Agent Rātana and I pulled up in the **ice-cream** van with the 'come and get your ice creams' music **BLARING**. I had offered to make it stop, but Agent Rātana had said no.

'He knows we're coming,' she said. 'Let's go full-noise.'

We got out and walked in between the empty rides towards the **TOWER OF TREMBLES**.

As we approached it, a big **black car** pulled
up. The Prime Minister and Major Flatly got out.

I did not expect that.

'Neither did I,' whispered Agent Rātana. **Oops.**
I was thinking out loud again.

'**Jason Mason**,' said the Prime
Minister. 'What are you doing here?'

'I wanted a **hot dog on a stick**
with tomato sauce,' I said.

'The **carnival** is closed,' said the
Prime Minister.

'My mistake,' I replied. 'What are you
doing here?'

This was a pretty **cheeky thing** to say
to the Prime Minister, but I figured I was in plenty of
trouble already.

'I am here because Major Flatly informed me there
was some **FUNNY** business going on. And it seems

there is — involving you two. Disobeying my orders, I'm sure. I'm not angry, I'm just disappointed.'

Ooh. That stung.

'Prime Minister—' said Agent Rātana

'Agent Rātana—' said the Prime Minister.

'SILENCE!' said a different but familiar voice.

At the same time all the lights on the carnival rides lit up one after another, with a sound like

DOOF DOOF DOOF.

I turned and saw Hugh Jarse beside the control panel for the **TOWER OF TREMBLES**. He was a holding a small remote.

'Who are you?' said the Prime Minister.

'I am Hugh Jarse,' said Hugh Jarse. 'And I'm in charge'.

'I don't think so,' said the Prime Minister. 'Major Flatly, sort out this reprobate.'

I should tell you that 'reprobate' is just a **FANCY**

word for '**baddie**'. (I had to look it up.) I should also tell you that two more things were about to happen that I definitely did not expect.

Major Flatly looked at the Prime Minister in a strange way and said, 'I'm afraid that's not going to happen.'

The Prime Minister said, 'I beg your pardon, Major Flatly!'

Right then, Major Flatly put his fingers under his collar and pulled off his face.

I mean to say, he pulled off the **RUBBER MASK** in the shape of Major Flatly's face that had been covering a completely different face.

'I'm not Major Flatly', said not-Major-Flatly. 'I am Lou Papèr.'

Lou Papèr! **THE DASTARDLY MASTER OF DISGUISE!**

I gasped.

Agent Rātana gasped.

The Prime Minister said, **'Oh, bum!'**

Then the Prime Minister said, 'Where is Major Flatly?'

'Tied up in your office in the Beehive,' said not-Major-Flatly, before laughing an EVIL laugh: 'A har har har!'

I recognised the sound of that laugh. It sounded a lot like **Hugh Jarse**'s laugh. Come to think of it, without any disguise at all Lou Papèr looked a lot like **Hugh Jarse**.

And then **Hugh Jarse** looked at Lou Papèr and said, 'Hello, sis!'

And Lou Papèr looked at **Hugh Jarse** and said, 'Hi, bro!'

Brother and sister!

'Not just brother and sister,' said **Hugh Jarse**. 'EVIL twins!'

I really had to stop thinking out loud. But they really were **EVIL** twins.

'Now, let's get on with our nefarious plans . . . I'm so glad you're here to see this, Prime Minister' said **Hugh Jarse**. 'Observe! At the top of the **TOWER OF TREMBLES!**'

Everyone turned and looked.

Just as I'd expected, at the very top of the **TOWER OF TREMBLES** was a black object about the size of a bucket, with lots of wires looping in and out of it and a big **'ON-OFF'** switch.

'From up there the density-specific particle beam **disintegrator** will destroy ever toilet bowl in Wellington, activated by this remote control.'

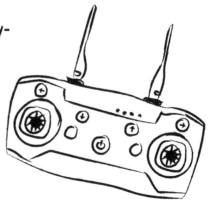

Hugh Jarse waved the little control in his hands.

'Or not,' he added, 'if **Jason Mason** gives me his invisibility ring!'

Yikes.

'What a terrible choice to have to make!' said **Hugh Jarse**, who was really getting into this **EVIL**-villain speech stuff. 'Leave the people of Wellington with nothing to go on, or grant me the power of invisibility!'

The Prime Minister, who seemed quite calm, said, 'I don't think so. The ring needs to be worn by someone related to **Jason's** Great Uncle Bill. DNA or something. It won't work for you.'

'I'll make it work for me!' **Hugh Jarse** snarled. 'I am an **EVIL** genius, remember? With an **EVIL** genius workshop in my **EVIL** genius headquarters? Oh yes, I will make it work for me.'

For once, the Prime Minister was lost for words.

There was a lot going on. I had to keep a clear head.

In the shadows behind the base of the **TOWER OF TREMBLES**, I could see Kyle. And Flight Lieutenant Dan. And my nana. That's right — my nana. She waved at me but I didn't wave back. I had a job to do. It was **SHOWTIME**.

I stepped forward and said, 'Wait just one minute!'

Hugh Jarse and the Prime Minister and Lou Papèr all turned and looked at me.

'I don't believe you! That thing up there, it's a fake, a hoax! That video in *Burgundy* was a **fake** and a hoax too. And we never actually saw that dense particular-thing—'

'Density-specific particle beam **disintegrator**,' Agent Rātana whispered in my ear.

'Yes, that,' I said. 'We never actually saw it work on top of the Eiffel Tower either. Because it's a **fake**!'

'I can assure you it is not a fake,' said **Hugh Jarse**.

'You tell him, brother!' said Lou Papèr.

'**Extraordinary** claims require extraordinary evidence!' I said.

'Ah-a, a Carl Sagan fan,' said **Hugh Jarse**. 'Very well. Let me give you a demonstration. It's the sort of thing us **EVIL** geniuses love to do. Now, I'm resetting the target density of the **disintegrator** to 'CHEAP LOW-QUALITY UNDERWEAR ELASTIC.'

He fiddled with some knobs on the remote control, then said **'Activation sequence starting**. Activating in five, four, three, two—'

There was a large **ZZZZZAP** sound from the top of the **TOWER OF TREMBLES**.

Suddenly, I felt my underpants **sag** under my shorts, as if the elastic holding them up had disappeared.

'**A har har har!**' laughed **Hugh Jarse**. 'I pity anyone wearing cheap low-quality underwear elastic today, **Jason Mason**!'

I looked around. No one else was having any problems. It seemed like they were all wearing expensive good-quality **undergarments**.

'So,' said **Hugh Jarse**, 'do you still doubt the power of the density-specific particle beam **disintegrator?**'

'But ... but ... how did you know?' I said.

'That you had cheap low-quality **undergarments?** I didn't. I just guessed. They're the sort of thing that a nobody like you would wear.'

A nobody. Nobody had called me a nobody since

Major Flatly had said it that time I was trying to save everyone at Eden Park from the world's most powerful **ITCHING** powder. And my mum had bought me those underpants with the money from her venetian-blind cleaning business.

Right then, I felt very cross and I wanted to call **Hugh Jarse** some of the words my dad had called the spare wheel from his old-style Volkswagen **Beetle** that time he dropped it on his foot. But I knew that wouldn't help, so I **bit my tongue**. Not *actually* bit it. That wouldn't have helped either.

'Now, give me the invisibility ring,' **Hugh Jarse** demanded.

I took a quick look at the base of the **TOWER OF TREMBLES**. All I could see was Kyle's hand giving a thumbs up then disappearing into the shadows.

It was time to wrap this up.

'You know I could make it to the top right now,' I said.

'You what?' **Hugh Jarse** scoffed. He looked at the empty seats at the bottom of the **TOWER OF TREMBLES**.

'You think,' he said, 'that you can run, jump on those seats, somehow get them going, ride them to the top and switch off the density-specific particle beam **disintegrator** before I can activate it?'

I stood as tall as I could, stared him in the eyes and said, 'Yes. I. Can.'

'I very much doubt that,' he said. 'But just in case you could . . .'

He pushed a button on the **TOWER OF TREMBLES** ride control panel. There was a **CLANK** and **WHIRR** and the empty seats slowly started moving up and up and up.

There was now no chance of me getting to the top.

'Now, give me the in𝕍isibility ring!' said

Hugh Jarse. 'In fact, give it to me before

those seats reach the top, or I will activate the

disintegrator. The clock is running now, **Jason**

Mason. The countdown is on. Ooh, I do like a

bit of drama.'

TOWER·OF
TREMBLES

I felt the ring on my finger.

'Don't do it,' said Agent Rātana.

The **empty seats** were now

halfway up the tower.

'I have to,' I said, 'otherwise . . .'

'That was your great uncle Bill's ring', said

Agent Rātana. 'He trusted you with it. He would

never let you give it away to these, these—'

'Almost there,' said **Hugh Jarse.**

'Don't want to hurry you.'

'Don't you dare, Jason!' said

Agent Rātana, 'What kind of person are you?'

'Hey, you're not my mother,' I snapped back.

The empty seats had reached the top of the
TOWER OF TREMBLES.

'Right, that's it,' said Hugh Jarse.
'Toilets away!'

'NO! WAIT!' I said, slipping the ring off my finger.
I handed it to Hugh Jarse and said, 'Here.
Take it.'

Right at that moment, my nana appeared sitting
in one of the empty seats at the very top of the
TOWER OF TREMBLES. It was as
if she had just been invisible, and now she
wasn't.

'Hello Jason!' she yelled down.

I leaned towards Hugh Jarse and said,
'By the way, I don't think that's the ring you want.'

I had given him a Burger Ring.

That's probably a lot for you to get your head around. **Believe me**, it was a lot for me to get my head around at the time. So, if you don't quite understand what's been going, let me explain . . .

You see, that little **argument** Agent Rātana and I just had, we didn't mean it. We were just acting. And me telling Hugh Jarse I could make it to the top of the **TOWER OF TREMBLES**. That was just me acting too. I knew I couldn't. And what I said about the **disintegrator** being a fake. I didn't mean that either.

It was all about distracting Hugh Jarse (and Lou Papèr too, as it turned out), getting them to look away from the bottom of the **TOWER OF TREMBLES**. Because that was where Kyle and Flight Lieutenant Dan were helping my nana get on one of the seats, so she could push the **BUTTON** on Great Uncle Bill's ring, which she was wearing (not me!) and go invisible. And so Kyle and Flight Lieutenant Dan could sneak back into the shadows.

I had thought of this right after Agent Rātana and I had had made up our list of assets and liabilities. I realised we had much more than an ice-cream van on our side. We had my nana! The invisibility ring would work for her, just like it worked for me. And she had always wanted to go on an adventure like her brother's.

And we had Kyle and Flight Lieutenant Dan, too.
They were always happy to help. Kyle knew my nana,
and Flight Lieutenant Dan knew how to drive. I gave
them Great Uncle Bill's ring, and they took it to
Twilight Views Rest Home and Villas, where they told

my nana the plan. And my nana

was, as she herself said, 'as keen as

mustard!'

Meanwhile, I needed a fake

ring to wear, so Agent Rātana

and I went and bought a packet

of **Burger Rings**. I found

one that looked good and ate

the rest.

And now we are back at the carnival. My
nana has just appeared at the top of the Tower
of Trembles, and Hugh Jarse has just
realised that he's been tricked.

My nana looked at the density-specific particle beam **disintegrator** beside her.

'Is this the thing I turn off?' she yelled.

'Yes!' I yelled back.

'What's going on?' said **Hugh Jarse**.

'Up or down?' yelled my nana.

'Up!' I **yelled**.

'Oh, no, she doesn't!' said **Hugh Jarse**.

He stabbed at the remote control with his finger.

'Activation in five, four—'

'It's quite stiff!' yelled my nana.

'You can do it, Nana!' I yelled back.

'Two, one—' shouted **Hugh Jarse**. And then . . .

Nothing.

No **ZZZZZAP** from the density-specific particle beam **disintegrator**.

No sound at all, except my nana saying,

'**Oooh, Jason**, I think I can see your house from here.'

She had done it! She had switched it off just in time.

No one else said anything. **Hugh Jarse**, Lou Papèr and the Prime Minister all looked stunned.

Agent Rātana whispered, 'Nice acting, Agent.'

Then the seats on the **TOWER OF TREMBLES** dropped to the ground, with my nana going **'Wahooo!'** all the way down.

Just then a taxi pulled up and Major Flatly got out. He had a short **argument** with the taxi driver, something about charging it back to the Ministry of Government Departments, then the taxi roared off.

'Good evening, Prime Minister. Sorry I'm late, I've been tied up,' said Major Flatly. 'Luckily, I escaped thanks to a **trick** taught to me by Agent Mason's great uncle Bill.'

Good old Great Uncle Bill!

'Agent Rātana, please accept my apologies for not believing you,' he continued.

'*Apology accepted*, Major,' said Agent Rātana.

'Wait, wait, wait!' said **Hugh Jarse**. 'This isn't over!'

'Ooh, I think it *is* over,' said Major Flatly. 'For you two, anyway. Listen — can you hear?'

I listened. I could hear helicopters, and cars, and s**i**r**c**n**s**, and a dog **barking**, and off in the distance a ship's horn.

'That's the Police, the Army, the Navy, the Air Force, the Diplomatic Protection Squad, the Dog Squad, the SAS, the SIS and the Coastguard,' said Major Flatly. 'They're coming from every direction, so there's no point trying to escape. **Hugh Jarse** and Lou Papèr, you're going to be spending a lot of time together'.

'Can I go on the ride again?' asked my nana.

209

And that is the end of the story of me and the
DASTARDLY MASTER OF DISGUISE.

Lou Papèr was put in **handcuffs** and helped
into a police van, followed by her brother. As he got
in, he looked over his shoulder and said, 'This isn't the
last you'll see of Hugh Jarse!'

I hoped he was wrong, just as I hoped we had seen
Lou Papèr's last role.

The density-specific particle beam
disintegrator was taken down from the top of the
TOWER OF TREMBLES and sent to

the **top-secret** government laboratory deep under Mount Victoria.

There it was given to Chief Science Officer **McNettles** (you might know her as Nettie) to analyse. Nettie later told me she was going to find out what else it could disintegrate, apart from **toilet bowls** and cheap underwear elastic.

Hopefully she can find out a way of using it for good instead of **EVIL**. I suggested that if she could make it disintegrate the **cauliflower** in my dad's casseroles that would be good. She said she would add that to the list.

My nana gave me a big kiss and said she had loved being part of a **secret agent** adventure like the ones her brother Bill used to go on.

She told the Prime Minister that the government was very LUCKY to have her grandson (me) as a **secret agent**.

The Prime Minister agreed but said it was important that my nana didn't tell anyone about what had happened.

My nana said not to worry as she was always forgetting things. She also said she might forget all this **secret agent** business more quickly if that nice young man could take her on outings from the Twilight Views Rest Home and Villas.

The Prime Minister and I — and everyone else — were confused about who the 'nice young man' was. It turns out she meant Major Flatly.

The Prime Minister thought this was an **excellent idea**. So, from then on, once a month on a Sunday afternoon, Major Flatly picks up my nana from the Twilight Views Rest Home and

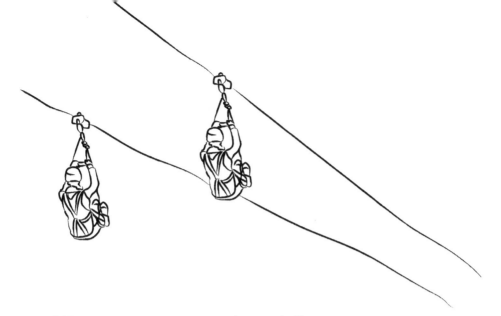

Villas and takes her on an 'outing'. This weekend they are having tea and scones with cream and jam and going ZIP-LINING.

The Prime Minister told Agent Rātana and me that the people of New Zealand would be **grateful** for all that we had done, if they had known what we had done, which they never would. But it was a nice thought.

The Prime Minister did not say anything more about Agent Rātana and me disobeying orders but did say that we were both '**undismissed**' and asked if we would be available for whenever there was a new mission.

Agent Rātana said yes, she would be, as long as it didn't happen in the next twenty-fours as she was going **cave abseiling**.

The Prime Minister said that sounded like a very **important** training exercise.

I was pretty sure it was another date with Flight Lieutenant Dan.

The next day, when the **carnival** was open to everybody (not just to **notorious** criminal masterminds, the prime minister, **secret agent**s and their friends and nanas), Kyle and I finally went on the **TOWER OF TREMBLES** together. It felt good to be just spending some time with my best friend.

The Prime Minister had thanked Kyle for his help in defeating Lou Papèr and **Hugh Jarse**.

Kyle had said that he wouldn't be forgetting that day for a long time and joked that maybe the Prime Minister should arrange for his MEMORY of it to be **ERASED**.

The Prime Minister told him that that could actually be arranged but it was probably against the law. I think that was also a **joke**.

My mind went back to that time in the Prime Minister's office when I'd thought for a second that Kyle and I would get to go on secret missions together. That would have been **amazing**.

When our seats reached the top of the **TOWER OF TREMBLES**, Kyle said, 'WOW!' and 'I can see your house from here!' and then a strange and unexpected thing happened.

A small *DRONE* appeared hovering in front of us, about two cubits from our faces. A little video screen

unfolded from it, and on that screen was Agent Rātana.

'Tēnā kōrua,' she said.

'Agent Rātana?' I said. 'You don't look like you're down a hole in the ground.'

'Change of plans,' she said. 'I'm driving towards you in the ice-cream van. Well, Flight Lieutenant Dan is driving and I'm on the phone. **Safety first**.'

'Hi guys!' said Flight Lieutenant Dan.

'Well, I'm confused,' I said.

'So am I,' said Kyle.

'We have a new **mission**,' said Agent Rātana. 'The Crown Prince of Berovnia is visiting New Zealand and we are on the security team.'

'Are we? Why?' I said.

'Because the Crown Prince of Berovnia is eleven years old,' said Agent Rātana.

Kyle and I looked at each other. Neither of us had ever heard of the Crown Prince of Berovnia, but we both nodded and made 'oh yes, that's right' sounds.

'And, of course,' Agent Rātana went on, 'he looks exactly like you, which will be very helpful.'

'Cool!' I said. 'A prince who looks exactly like me . . .'

'No, not you,' said Agent Rātana. 'Kyle. He looks exactly like Kyle.'

Kyle and I looked at each other with **wide** eyes. Did this mean . . .?

'So, we'll all be working together on this one,' said Agent Rātana. 'We'll be there in twenty-five seconds to pick you both up and give you the full **mission** briefing. See you at the bottom.'

There was a sound of 'come and get your ice creams' music in the distance. Kyle and I saw the **ice-cream van** approaching along the road towards the carnival.

Then we dropped down — fast.

Wahoooooo!

THE END

ALSO IN THE SERIES

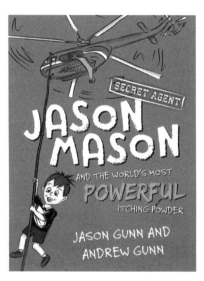